THE YOUTH ELIXIR

CINDY KIRK

WAVERLY
HOUSE

ISBN: 9798322875130

CHAPTER ONE

"I bid seven." Matilda "Til" Beemis glanced at the cards in her hand and hid a smile. Her luck had finally turned. Even though seven was a stretch—with only an ace and a queen—if she got the trey, she'd be more than halfway to her bid.

She and her friends had gathered for lunch, cards and conversation. Today, the game was Pitch. They'd decided to play the version Call for Your Partner, a favorite of Til's.

Geraldine Walker shook her head. "I can't go eight."

"I can't even go five." Beverly Raymond placed her cards face down on the table and heaved an exaggerated sigh.

Neither of the other two at the table in Geraldine and Beverly's dining room was willing to take a chance and bid higher.

Til's lips curved in satisfaction. Though she wasn't positive she could get seven, she decided to embrace the mindset—go bold or go home.

"The bid is yours, Til. What are you looking for?" Lisa Rogan, the youngest of the five friends, shot a quick glance at the cards in her hands. No doubt wondering if she'd be Til's partner for this hand.

Although Lisa was only fifty, decades younger than the other four women, Lisa had an "old soul" and fit in perfectly.

"Spades." Til laid down her ace. "I'm calling for the three."

Directly across the table, Rosemary Woodsen grimaced. When it came her turn to lay down her card, she placed the three of spades on the pile. "I'm afraid that's the only help I can give."

Til might have groaned on the inside, but she shot Rosemary a reassuring smile. "No worries."

The truth was, Til had counted on her partner helping her reach seven. Now she was going to have to make it on her own. At least she was in familiar territory—she'd been on her own most of her life.

Unfortunately, this time if she failed, she wouldn't be the only one who went down in flames. She would take Lisa down with her.

Think positive, Til told herself.

But when Geraldine's lips curved, Til knew even a positive attitude wasn't going to save her. Or Lisa.

After cards, the women moved outside for cookies and lemonade. It had been only two hours since they'd each enjoyed a red velvet cupcake with thick cream cheese topping for dessert.

No one appeared bothered by that, especially when Beverly announced she'd stopped by the bakery that morning and picked up a dozen Berger cookies. The soft cakelike cookies with a mound of rich fudge frosting were irresistible and had been a Maryland favorite for nearly two hundred years.

Talk on the porch quickly turned to a favorite topic—Rosemary's upcoming wedding. Love had come late in life to the handsome woman with the long gray braid down her back. Not long after arriving in town, Rosemary had met Barry Whitehead and fallen head over heels.

"You two make such a cute couple," Beverly gushed.

"Barry is wonderful." A soft look filled Rosemary's blue eyes. "I feel like I'm getting a do-over in life. Not that my life hasn't been good," Rosemary quickly added. "I'm so lucky to have Jenna and now Daniel."

Rosemary had moved to GraceTown with her great-niece, who had also found a love of her own.

Expelling a happy sigh, Rosemary reached for another cookie. "Marrying the man I love makes me feel, well, I feel like I'm getting to try out life the way I once thought it would be. Who wouldn't want that?"

Beverly and Geraldine exchanged a glance. Both in their seventies, they'd shared a home for close to fifty years. Happy with the life they'd built, they seemed to have escaped the concern with marital status, unlike many women Til had grown up with.

Pretty ribbons of silver threaded through Beverly's light brown hair. As long as Til could remember, the retired RN had worn her hair in a soft coil at the nape of her neck.

Geraldine, her hair short and straight, had always marched to her own beat. She was unapologetically handy with tools and engines, skills Til envied.

For years, whenever Til or one of her friends needed help with anything—be it a sputtering car or a stopped-up sink—Geraldine got the call.

"I wouldn't change a thing." Geraldine's gaze settled on Beverly, and for a moment, a soft look filled her eyes.

Beverly smiled back. "No do-over for me either. I've been blessed with a happy life and wouldn't risk changing a thing."

"Sometimes life forces you to change." Lisa spoke for the first time since the discussion had begun. "Whether you want to or not."

Til assumed her friend was referring to when she'd been diagnosed with multiple sclerosis and her husband had left her while she was in the ICU during an MS relapse.

"Tom is a jerk." Geraldine spoke what each of them was thinking.

"The thing is, lots of people viewed my diagnosis and divorce as the end of my life." Lisa lifted her crystal tumbler of lemonade and took a sip. "For a moment, I did, too. Then Charlie came home, Hannah moved to town, and like Rosemary, I was given a fresh start."

Beverly inclined her head. "I'm afraid you lost me."

"I'm finally living the life I wanted but never got. Actually, I'm living the life I never even knew I wanted, because I can tell you that when Charlie was a teenager, I wasn't exactly hoping he'd live with me forever." Lisa gave a little laugh. "I'm not saying my life doesn't have challenges, but it still feels like a gift."

Geraldine's gaze turned serious as she chewed on the words. "Is it really a new life or just part of your journey?"

"That's what I was wondering, too." Beverly slanted a glance at Geraldine, before shifting her attention back to Lisa. "The MS and the divorce resulted in lots of changes in your life, but you never stopped being the Lisa we all know and love."

A thoughtful look crossed Lisa's face as she bit into a cookie. She shrugged. "You may be right."

"What about you, Til?" Rosemary asked. "Would you want a do-over?"

"Honestly, I'm not sure." Normally, Til was quick to voice an opinion. Not this time.

The conversation had taken her thoughts down a road she rarely traveled. She'd never contemplated a life in which her parents didn't die young, or her fiancé didn't leave her, because what would be the point? Dreaming of something different wouldn't change anything.

Besides, she had good friends and a sense of purpose in life. That was more than most people had.

Yet, at the same time, hearing her friends talk about the idea of a do-over stirred something inside Til.

It would be nice to know there was still plenty of time to discover new people and experiences, rather than to feel like all those opportunities were in the rearview.

Til wondered if who she was now had been forged by the challenges she'd encountered over the past nine decades. Would she be different if she'd been presented with different experiences and opportunities?

"C'mon, Til," Beverly teased when the silence lengthened. "You have to have an opinion. You always do."

Til offered a rueful smile. "The thing is, when you're north of ninety like me, while you might have the desire for the new, there's no point in pretending you've got the time."

Instead of driving to the card party, Til had walked. When it came time to leave, she turned down Rosemary's offer to drive her home and saw herself out.

Holding on to the rail, she carefully navigated the porch steps, then paused on the sidewalk outside the stately Victorian. Til found herself in no hurry to head home to an empty house...alone.

Why did that single word have her mood suddenly plummeting? She'd lived alone for most of her life and regarded her bungalow in the Maplewood Village area of GraceTown as her sanctuary.

Til sighed. This melancholy wasn't like her. Neither was her current indecision about where to go and what to do now that the card party had ended. Especially on a lovely summer day when the sun shone bright in a cloudless sky of brilliant blue.

She thought of the recently released novel that she'd eagerly anticipated reading for months. She didn't have the slightest doubt that sitting on her porch glider with that book would have her mood sunny in no time.

The book nestled in her handbag had Til quickening her steps in the direction of home. Halfway there, she changed course. Instead of turning right—which would have taken her to her front door—she impulsively turned left, in the direction of Maplewood Park.

Though eager to start reading, Til deliberately slowed her pace and reminded herself that life was a journey to be savored, not gulped.

A middle-aged woman with hair turning to silver straightened from the mulch she was adding around a large maple and flashed a smile. "You've got the right idea. It's a perfect afternoon for a walk."

Til knew Sally Hardy from the tutoring program for inmates at the local detention center. Like Til, Sally was a former teacher who believed strongly in the importance of literacy.

Gesturing with one hand to Sally's yard, Til smiled. "It's also a gorgeous day for yard work."

"Yes, it is." The woman laughed. "Though not nearly as much fun as a stroll."

After a few minutes of conversation, Til continued on her way. Over the years, she'd watched the home that Sally and her husband had purchased go from dilapidated to showstopping gorgeous. The two-bedroom bungalow boasted a fresh coat of paint, new shutters and a yard that was the envy of the neighborhood.

The Maplewood Village area had experienced a resurgence in recent years when affordable housing in GraceTown had become nearly out of reach for most working-class families. Long-neglected homes in the area had been purchased by those who weren't intimidated by fixer-uppers, as Til had heard the pretty lady on TV call them.

The park came into view, and Til quickened her steps, eager to take a seat on her favorite bench and crack open the book.

Familiar with the surroundings, she barely noticed the large crack in the wooden sign shaped like a tree, announcing this was Maplewood Park. The park had aged as badly as the sign, the playground area offering only a sad-looking metal slide, a broken merry-go-round and three u-shaped rubber swings.

The wooden benches scattered around the park were just as weathered, the metal holding the boards in place showing ample rust. Still, Til shivered with anticipation and picked up her pace.

Her favorite bench at the back of the park provided everything she needed—a place to sit, partial shade thanks to a leafy maple and a stand of hollyhocks.

Hollyhocks had been her dad's favorite flower. Each time she saw the tall spikes of colorful flowers, she thought of him. Though he'd been gone longer than he'd been in her life, her dad remained alive in her memory.

After her mother died when she was nine, Til's father became her entire world. Not once had he given her cause to doubt his love. He—

Til came to an abrupt halt, what she was seeing putting a stop to her trip down memory lane.

In all the years she'd been coming here, Til had never seen anyone else sit on this particular bench.

Much less someone so young and vibrant.

The woman's dark hair sported red streaks that matched the color of her lipstick. Her yellow shorts showed off long, tanned legs, and the white sleeveless shirt drew the eye to the tree of life tattoo on her bicep.

Til knew the symbol's significance. She especially loved the part about remaining strong despite trials and hardships.

She wondered if that sentiment was why this young woman had chosen the tat. Curious, but not wanting to intrude, since the woman appeared lost in thought, Til silently began to back up.

There were other benches in the park where she could sit and read, or she could simply head home.

"Don't go." The woman, her blue eyes appearing almost violet in the light, focused on Til. She motioned her forward. "Please, join me."

Something in the woman's smile had Til halting her retreat and stepping to the bench.

When Til drew close, the woman rose with easy grace. She extended her hand in a curiously formal gesture. "Good afternoon. I'm Serena Nordine."

Til took the hand with its shiny gold nails and gave it a firm shake. "Matilda Beemis. Everyone calls me Til."

"What a beautiful name. Matilda." The woman rolled the name around on her tongue as if savoring the taste of it, then flashed a smile and gestured with one hand to the blue sky. "Isn't it a peach of a day?"

The expression that Til hadn't heard since she'd been a girl made her smile. She liked that these old expressions were making a comeback.

When Serena resumed her seat on the bench and gestured for her to sit, Til sat beside her.

"You're right. The day is absolutely gorgeous." Til studied the young woman. "Do you live around here?"

"I've lived a lot of places."

A woman of few words. Til understood. Her friends had told her that nowadays you had to be careful about how much information you shared with strangers.

"You don't need to be careful with me."

Serena's comment had Til's eyes widening. Was she that transparent?

"I realize this sounds crazy, but I trust you." Til gave a little laugh. "Something about you is familiar."

Serena's violet eyes—there really was no other way to

describe them—searched Til's face. "How has your day been so far?"

"It's been grand." Til's use of the word from her childhood had Serena smiling and Til elaborating. "I had lunch, then played cards with friends. One of the ladies will be marrying soon. There was much joy in the air when we spoke of her upcoming nuptials."

"And perhaps a little sorrow?"

Puzzled by the odd comment, Til pulled her brows together. "What do you mean?"

"Your life has not followed the course you assumed it would." Serena's gaze turned thoughtful. "You once dreamed of a life with a husband. It was, after all, what was expected of most women in the 1940s."

Though it had to be simply a good guess, Serena spoke the truth. While marriage and children were no longer the course in life that all modern women dreamed of, when Til had been in her twenties, marriage followed by children had been every young girl's dream.

When Vince had returned from WWII and they'd met and fallen in love, Til's future had seemed to be headed down the traditional path.

Not meant to be, Til reminded herself. After all these years, thoughts of Vince no longer brought an ache to her heart. Perhaps a bit of wistfulness for what might have been, but that was all.

She glanced down at her wrinkled hands, then farther to her serviceable shoes and smiled ruefully. Okay, she could admit—but only to herself—that she sometimes experienced a pang of envy when seeing a couple in love or a young woman with her whole life spread out before her like a pretty quilt.

Still, she'd never been one to dwell on what couldn't be changed. At the grand old age of ninety-two, she wasn't about to start now. She'd made the most of the life she'd been given. When life had given her lemons, she'd made lemonade.

Serena's steady gaze had Til realizing the young woman was waiting for a response. "Yes, I've remained single. I've had a good life."

"You've helped migrant seasonal workers learn to read." Admiration shone in Serena's eyes. "You've also helped local residents with low literacy skills."

"I was a teacher. I enjoy opening the world to adults and children through books." Til's lips tipped up. Then the smile faded as a thought struck. "How is it you know so much about me?"

Serena waved an airy hand. "You're practically a local celebrity."

Til hooted out a laugh. "Hardly."

"You continue to volunteer."

"Not as much as I once did, but yes, I enjoy serving my community." *Enough about me,* Til thought. "What is it you do, Serena?"

"Jobwise or in general?"

"Both."

"I think of myself as someone who dispenses gifts to those who have earned a reward."

Til shifted on the wooden bench. "I'm afraid I don't understand."

"I have something for you." Serena's gaze remained steady on Til's face. "Call it a reward for a life well-lived."

A squirrel chattered in a nearby tree while a bee landed on a hollyhock flower. Though leafy branches shaded the bench from the full heat of the sun, the day was warm. Nevertheless, Til experienced a sudden chill.

"I don't need a reward." She moved to rise, but Serena's hand on her arm had her resuming her seat.

"You don't need to be afraid of me or what I'm offering." Serena's voice was as warm as her hand. "Whether to accept the gift or refuse it is your choice."

Reaching into her bag, Serena pulled out an ornate bottle containing a small amount of purplish liquid.

Intrigued, Til leaned forward for a better look. "The bottle is gorgeous."

"Here." Serena handed it to her.

Holding it securely, Til carefully tipped the bottle from side to side. There wasn't as much liquid in it as she'd first thought—no more than two ounces.

Initially, she would have sworn the liquid was purple, but it now appeared pink. As she continued to stare, the color changed again, this time to a pretty blue.

"The bottle is lovely, and the way the liquid changes color is fascinating." Til glanced at Serena and asked, "What's in it?"

"You have a curious mind. It's one of the things I admire about you." Serena smiled, then her expression sobered. "This is going to be difficult for you to believe, so I need to request that you hear me out before you ask questions or offer comments. Can you do that?"

Til thought of the book in her purse and suppressed a sigh. It appeared she wasn't going to get any reading done, at least not until she got home. But she had to admit that Serena's words and the bottle fired her curiosity.

What could the woman have to say? Was she hawking some kind of vitamin supplement or energy drink? Or was it a sample of a healthy cocktail Serena had concocted? There appeared to be only one way to find out.

She would listen.

CHAPTER TWO

"I will hear you out." Til held out the bottle to Serena. "Without interrupting."

The young woman waved a hand. "Keep it for now."

Til tightened her hold on the bottle. "Tell me."

"In your hands, you hold something very special—a youth elixir. If you drink it, you will be young again. You will have the chance to live your life again, with all the knowledge and wisdom you have gleaned over the past nine decades."

A youth elixir? It took everything in Til not to laugh aloud. She glanced around, expecting to see a kid videoing this as part of some social media prank. "Who put you up to this?"

"It's not what you think." Serena spoke in the same matter-of-fact tone. "You need to understand that your aged body will die. You will lose access to your current worldly possessions and will start over completely on your own. You can choose a new name, and you will be given a new identity with a new background and papers to prove who you are. What you choose to do with this new life will be entirely up to you."

Til knew her hearing wasn't what it once was, but she had

been paying attention. She searched Serena's face. "Are you serious?"

"Very." A light glimmered in Serena's eyes. "You have spent your life caring for others, Matilda. This is a reward, a chance for you to, well, begin again."

"I don't know what to say." Til brought a trembling hand to her head to brush back a strand of hair that had gone cloud-white decades earlier.

When she'd been young, her hair had been the color of walnut, shiny and dark.

"It's rare for someone to be given this opportunity." Serena's violet eyes searched her face. "You're a special woman, Matilda Beemis."

There it was, that sense of déjà vu, as if she knew Serena, or had known her at one time. That fact, accompanied by the feeling that she could trust her, had Til's gaze dropping to the bottle she held.

What if Serena spoke the truth? GraceTown was certainly known for unexplainable happenings. Til had actually witnessed a couple of those events herself.

Could this be one of them? Her pulse quickened. What would it be like to be young again? To be free to do all the things she'd never had the opportunity to do? To travel and dance, to date like other young women and perhaps even fall in love?

Then she remembered the downside.

"You're saying drinking this will kill me." Til found herself surprised at how calm she sounded.

"The shell that is currently your body will die." Serena gestured with one hand toward her youthful frame. "That body will be replaced by a young one, like mine."

Til thought of the family and friends who'd passed through her life, people she loved, people she'd grieved. She had no family left. Now, at ninety-two, all her friends were younger. How many more years did she have left anyway?

That fact had been brought home this afternoon as she'd listened to her friends talk about their futures. She hadn't said much, knowing she had, at most, a handful of years left.

Her gaze dropped to the bottle.

"You mentioned I'll only have the clothes on my back." Ever the pragmatist, Til considered the profound difficulty of starting over with absolutely nothing. "That will make it nearly impossible for me to function and survive."

Serena's lips curved up in a slight smile. "I believe you know in your heart where to find what you need."

Well, that was hardly helpful.

"What name would you like?" Serena asked.

Til blinked. "Name?"

"You can no longer be Matilda Beemis," Serena gently reminded her. "I need a new name for the papers."

Another reminder that Matilda Beemis would cease to exist. Perhaps twenty years ago, maybe even ten, Til might have hesitated. But she'd come to grips with the fact that she was near the end of her life and had released any lingering dreams out into the ether.

Right now, it was time to focus on practicalities. "What papers will you be giving me?"

"Driver's license, Social Security card, passport, birth certificate, résumé." Serena rattled the items off without hesitation. "What you do with what you're given will be up to you."

Til thought back to Serena's cryptic comment. "You believe I'll know how to survive."

"I believe you'll know where to find whatever you need."

Til might have found Serena's confidence touching if she hadn't been so perplexed. While she knew everything didn't always need to make sense, it didn't stop the questions. "How did you find me in this park when I didn't even plan to come here?"

Serena smiled. "You love to come to the park on beautiful days."

True enough, Til supposed. "Why you?"

Serena's eyes widened. She appeared startled by the question. "What do you mean?"

Til shifted, hoping to find a more comfortable spot on the bench. She didn't have much meat on her bones, and for some reason, the bench seemed more unforgiving than usual this afternoon. "Why are you the one offering me this? Is that what you do? Go around dispensing do-overs?"

Serena shook her head. "Awarding this type of gift is rare. I'm here because you're special."

Til nearly snorted out a laugh, something her father would have dubbed very unladylike. An ache lanced her heart. Even after all these years, she missed her papa. He'd been such a good man, such an amazing father.

"I'm not—special, I mean." Til thought back over her life. Her mother dying when she was nine. Papa stepping up to be both father and mother. Working side by side with him at the hotel he owned. Caring for him when he became ill. Going to college, working and volunteering. "I didn't have a family, so I had the time to help others."

Serena leaned forward, her expression earnest. "You might think that, but we all have choices in how we live our life. You have built a remarkable legacy that will be remembered long after you're gone."

"That's kind of you to say—"

"Not just kind, true. This can be your chance, your time, to explore and experience all the world has to offer. The world will be your oyster." Serena offered a supportive smile. "I believe there is nothing you can't conquer if you put your mind to it and aim high."

The words struck a chord in her memory, as if she'd heard them sometime before. The remembrance hovered just out of reach, but she didn't push too hard to find it. Right now, the focus was on looking ahead, not behind.

For a second, it seemed as if the world around her held its collective breath, awaiting her decision. The squirrel ceased chattering, the bee froze on the hollyhock flower, and the slight breeze stilled.

Til's heart began an erratic rhythm, speeding up like a runaway locomotive, then slowing so severely she wondered if it beat at all.

She thought about her friends, how it would be to interact with them as her new self. This wouldn't really be a loss for them. It'd be like what they'd all been talking about—a new start.

One that she'd never be able to experience without this opportunity.

Decision made, Til lifted the bottle and would have drunk the liquid right then, but Serena put a restraining hand on her arm.

"What?" Til asked. "Did you change your mind?"

Til was no stranger to getting to the trough and not being allowed to drink. It had been that way with Vince. She'd been so close to being his bride when everything had fallen apart.

"I need your new name, the one you will be using from now on." A twinkle filled Serena's violet eyes. "Choose carefully. This will be your identity for the rest of your life. Once you decide, there is no changing it."

Til had spent nearly a century as Matilda Beemis. She liked her name, but it seemed fitting to start this second chapter in her life with a new one.

Unlike many she knew, Til had never been great at coming up with pithy comments or smart retorts on the fly. She wished she had a day or two to consider what name to choose. Then again, the more time she had to consider Serena's proposition, the more likely she'd get cold feet.

But she didn't have forty-eight hours. Serena needed her answer now.

Bringing a finger to her lips, Til thought of the Daniel Grace novel she'd finished last night. Emily had been an admirable female protagonist, while Curtis had been a main character who'd grown by leaps and bounds during the course of the book. By the end, she'd found herself rooting for the guy. As she found it difficult to think of any other names at this moment, she met Serena's gaze. "My name will be Emily Curtis."

"A fine choice." Serena smiled and handed her a manila envelope. "Your papers are in there. Oh, and don't forget your violin."

Serena lifted the case from where it sat at her feet and placed it beside Til.

"I don't play the violin," Til protested.

"Matilda Beemis didn't," Serena gently corrected. "Emily Curtis is a concert violinist."

Til blinked. "What am I now?"

"Whatever you want to be." Serena smiled. "Once you drink the elixir."

With fingers that trembled only slightly, Til lifted the ornate bottle, amazed by the way the elixir shimmered in the soft afternoon light.

Her gaze shifted to Serena, who sat watching her with an intense expression. She'd offered her this do-over, but wouldn't push.

Til downed the liquid in one gulp.

The taste reminded her of the mulberries that had once grown wild in the backyard when she'd been a child.

That was her last thought before everything went black.

CHAPTER THREE

Opening her eyes, Til blinked against the brightness of the sun. Though uncertain how much time had passed, she realized that she was no longer in Maplewood Park, but sitting at the base of the Angel of GraceTown statue.

Though the angel was a popular tourist attraction, today no one else was in this area of the town square. Instead of the floral dress and serviceable shoes Til had worn to the card party, she now wore sneakers, a stretchy kind of jean fabric for pants and a sleeveless top in an eye-popping blue.

Til reached up to touch the strand of hair that the wind blew in her face. The color was no longer cloud-white, nor the dark brown of her youth, but a pretty honey blond.

Her heart gave a solid thump against her chest. Was she hallucinating? Was this some kind of drug trip?

Scrambling to her feet, she moved her shoulders and legs and realized the aches and pains that had become her constant companion the last few years were gone.

She stretched and extended her fingers, noticing the age spots and wrinkles were gone. No, this felt too real to be a hallucination. On the outside, and at the core, she was different.

Eager to see if she looked as young as she felt, Til glanced down, expecting to see her pocketbook, which had a tiny mirror nestled in one of the side pockets.

Instead, there was only the manila envelope and violin case that Serena had given her. Ignoring the violin, Til opened the envelope and pulled out the contents.

Along with her book, the official documents that Serena had promised were there. For a long moment, Til studied the picture of Emily on the driver's license.

Instead of an old woman, a young woman smiled back at her. So pretty. So incredibly young. So different.

Til studied the picture even more closely. Was this really how she looked now? No way to know until she found a mirror.

Grabbing the violin case and the envelope, she considered next steps. Having identification was all well and good, but that wouldn't get her a place to stay or fill a belly that would soon want food.

What had Serena said to her? Something about her knowing how to find what she would need?

The bank was clearly out. She didn't have the necessary identification. If she attempted to withdraw money from an old woman's account, a bank where she had done business for half a century, she would likely be arrested.

Heck, if they'd already found her body in the park, that would make her attempt to withdraw funds even more suspicious.

Her lips quirked up in a wry smile. In a way, she did have something to do with it. She had, after all, drunk the liquid that had ended Matilda Beemis and birthed Emily Curtis.

Enough silliness. The sky overhead had turned dark, and she had enough experience with the weather in this part of the country to know when a storm was moving in.

First things first.

Money for food and a place to stay.

One raindrop plopped on the ground before her. Then another.

From the time she'd been a little girl, Papa had stressed the importance of setting aside money for a rainy day.

Not in a bank, because banks could fail. He'd been a young man when the stock market had crashed in 1929. That was why he'd always had cash set aside in a coffee can hidden in the house.

Til had not experienced a bank failure, but she'd followed his lead and kept a healthy sum of cash in the same coffee can he'd once used. She stored it in the lean-to at the back of her house, in the area where she kept her gardening supplies.

Unless a person knew where it was, they'd never find it.

Taking it wouldn't be stealing. It was her money, hard-earned and set aside for a rainy day.

As Til glanced up at the once-blue sky now gone dark, thunder rumbled. If this wasn't a rainy day, she didn't know what would qualify.

Glancing up at the sky one more time, Til took off running. Even as the rain began to fall, joy filled her as she realized she was actually able to run.

Not wanting to draw the attention of neighbors who might wonder about a stranger standing on Matilda Beemis's front porch, Til entered the property from the back alley.

The key was right where she'd hidden it, on the underside of the kitchen window, held in place by a thin wire. Opening the back door, she stepped inside and stood there, breathing in the familiar scent of rosemary, thyme and mint emanating from the herb garden in the pots on the shelves in this utility area.

This was her house, the place she'd loved and made a home. For a moment, the realization of all that had changed had tears springing to her eyes.

With one sip of the youth elixir, her days of puttering in her garden, of clipping herbs for a special dish or to add flavor to a salad had ended. That had been Til's life.

She was Emily now.

Had she made a mistake? Even as she crouched down and pushed aside clay pots and gardening tools, she felt a pang of, well, something.

Not regret, but sadness over the friends and things—like this house—that she would leave behind.

Her searching fingers found the coffee can, the bills covered by dozens of rags, some holding the faint smell of peat moss. She pulled out the can and set it on a drop-leaf table that had seen better days.

She was glancing around for a canvas bag where she could place the cash and the important papers when she remembered the letters.

Those, she would not leave behind.

Inside the quiet home where the scent of cinnamon lingered from the monkey bread she'd baked yesterday, Til found not only the canvas tote, but the letters bound with a pretty lavender ribbon.

She also found a mirror.

The young woman who stared back looked nothing like her. Her dark hair was now the honey-blond that her favorite movie star had once sported, a color she'd envied. Even her eye color had changed—brown had become blue.

After casting one last look in the mirror, Til carefully placed the letters in the tote—along with the envelope Serena had given her—then slipped out the back door.

She stood for a moment, silently offering a good-bye to the home that had given her shelter for so many years.

This clapboard house had been where she'd dreamed so many dreams over the years. There had been one dream in particular that had recurred numerous times.

A man waiting for her, his heart filled with love and his arms outstretched.

The man wasn't Vince. Til had quit pining for him long ago. This was someone else. Occasionally, when she was having difficulty falling asleep, she would think of the man, and sometimes she would feel his arms closing around her.

Though the encounter gave her comfort, Til never mentioned him to her friends. It seemed the kind of fantasy more suited to a young girl than a mature woman.

Til hadn't chosen to drink the liquid because of a dream of finding her fantasy man, but because of how she felt right now.

Her body was young and agile again, her brain firing on all cylinders. The future stretched out before her, offering a life that was hers for the taking.

Emily Curtis had no responsibilities beyond herself. Not that Til regretted caring for her father after his stroke or having limited choices in a career.

When she'd been young, there had been only three choices open to women—teacher, nurse, housewife.

As a teacher, she'd built a good life for herself.

Now, the opportunities were endless.

Til hefted the canvas bag over her shoulder and lifted the violin case. All was good. She had enough money to tide her over.

It was now time to find a place to stay.

The Graceful Oasis Hotel, located in GraceTown's historic district, had literally risen from the ashes of a previous business after the interior was gutted by fire in the 1990s. When that owner decided to take the insurance money and relocate his business elsewhere, a young entrepreneur named Ken Edwards had seen the possibilities.

He'd purchased the building with its downstairs camera shop

and handful of small studio apartments upstairs and repurposed the space into a quaint boutique hotel.

The way it was now, with a main-level kitchen and communal eating area, reminded Til of a B&B masquerading as a hotel. It had been a charming addition to this area of downtown.

Rates were reasonable, and the rooms were usually full, at least according to Chloe.

Chloe.

Til put one foot in front of the other, the hotel now in sight. Her heart sighed at the thought of Chloe. She would miss all her friends, but Chloe, well, Chloe was like family.

Twenty years ago, Til's path had crossed with Chloe's mother at a community event. She and Inez Patrick had begun talking, and a connection had formed. Neither Inez nor her husband had family in the area, and somehow Til had ended up becoming a de facto grandmother to seven-year-old Chloe.

When Inez and Forrest had begun traveling more for their business, Til had stepped up to help. Either Til would stay at Chloe's house, or Chloe would stay with her.

The day Chloe left for college had been a sad one for Til. Then her parents had moved to Paris, which meant that Chloe hadn't come back to GraceTown as often.

Earlier this year, after working in Miami for several years after college, Chloe had unexpectedly returned to GraceTown. The young woman had been so busy getting settled the past few months that Til hadn't seen much of her. She'd been looking forward to rekindling their bond.

Now, hopefully she would start a new friendship with Chloe as Emily.

Stepping up to the shiny mahogany desk in the hotel lobby, Til felt her heart slam against her ribs. She flashed a smile at Chloe.

"Welcome to the Oasis." Chloe's wavy brown hair tumbled

around her shoulders, and the smile on her red lips was reflected in her amber eyes. "How may I help you?"

Not a single flicker of recognition. Not that Til had expected any. "I was wondering if you have a room for one available?"

"How many nights?"

Though Til didn't know the exact rate for a room at the Oasis, she needed a home base until she secured permanent lodging. "Two weeks?"

Chloe's brows pulled together as she studied the computer screen. "For one guest?"

"Yes."

Chloe nodded as her gaze returned to the screen. Then she looked up and smiled. "You're in luck. We have one room, a lovely one on the top floor. The space can only accommodate a twin bed, which is why it is available. It's..."

The amount Chloe quoted had Til's mouth going dry. "That much?"

"Let me see what I can do." A look of understanding crossed Chloe's face. "For a two-week stay, paid up front, I can reduce the total to..."

The figure she named was definitely a savings, though not as much of a discount as Til had hoped.

Til nodded. "I'll take it."

"What is the name?"

For a second, Til hesitated. "Emily Curtis."

"I'll need to see a credit card and a photo ID, please."

Reaching into her tote, Til pulled out the driver's license and enough money to cover the entire stay.

"I don't have a credit card." Til let the statement hang out there for several seconds. Over the years, she'd learned the importance of simply stating facts. "I promise I won't trash the room."

Chloe studied her face for a long time, reminding Til of how she'd studied Serena's earlier. "We normally require a credit card on file, but I think we can make an exception this time."

Smiling, Chloe handed Til her change and the license, then pulled out an old-fashioned brass key. Chloe slid it across the counter to Til, along with a paper jacket. "There's a sheet with the breakfast hours and the Wi-Fi password. I hope you enjoy—"

"Chloe. Did you hear?" A slender young woman, her jet-black hair in a layered pixie cut, raced into the lobby, then skidded to a stop.

"Jaclyn, could you give me a minute?" Chloe smiled at the young woman, her tone easy. "I'm with a guest."

"I'm so sorry." Jaclyn shot Til an apologetic look before returning her gaze to Chloe. "But it's all over the news. They found your friend Matilda Beemis. The police are investigating."

Chloe whirled. "What do you mean 'found' her?"

"A woman walking her dog found her in Maplewood Park." Sympathy filled Jaclyn's eyes. "On a park bench."

"Was she injured? Is she okay?" Worry filled Chloe's amber eyes.

Jaclyn cast a glance at Emily, then stepped close to Chloe and lowered her voice. Despite the effort, Jaclyn had a voice that carried.

Even as she pretended to study the sheet detailing the breakfast and happy-hour times, Emily had no trouble hearing every word.

"I'm sorry, Chloe. She's dead." Jaclyn put a hand on Chloe's shoulder. "She was just sitting there. Her purse was beside her. Everything appeared to be in it. Word is that it doesn't appear she was assaulted."

Tears slipped down Chloe's cheeks, and an answering ache filled Emily's heart. She strode to the elevator and stepped inside, no longer able to witness the grief she'd caused.

Choices, she'd learned long ago, came with consequences. Her father had always warned her to think carefully about any decisions she made, saying that choices, like a stone thrown into a pond, created ripples that touched everything around.

Emily consoled herself that she had given this particular choice careful consideration.

As soon as Emily reached her room, she dropped the tote on the bed and moved straight to the mirror in the bathroom. A stranger gazed back at her.

No one would recognize her—heck, she didn't even recognize herself. She hadn't thought to ask Serena if she would look like her younger self or someone else, or if she had a choice in the matter. The outer shell might have changed, but inside, she was still her.

"Emily," she murmured, keeping her gaze firmly fixed on the image in the glass. "Emily Curtis."

Odd, the name chosen in such short order appeared to not only fit her, but it felt natural on her tongue.

The change had actually happened. Just as Serena had said it would. But not without casualties.

Tears flooded her eyes as she thought of the grief on Chloe's face. There was not a doubt in her mind that once news got out, Chloe wouldn't be the only who would grieve.

She hadn't wanted to leave her friends behind, but in reality, the end of her life had been just around the corner. By drinking what she thought of as the youth elixir, she'd only hastened the inevitable.

Brushing away the tears, Emily took a deep, steadying breath and glanced around the room that would be her home for the next two weeks.

The bed, covered in a quilt with a bright green and yellow daffodil pattern, brought a smile to her lips. Everything else in the small room was equally lovely. Seeing a claw-foot tub in the bathroom delighted her. She envisioned soaking up to her neck in bubbles while enjoying a glass of wine with music in the background.

She would make that happen. Later, she would cap off the first day of her new life with bubbles and wine.

Afterward, she would do some serious thinking about her future—where she would live, where she would work and what she would do with the rest of this new, glorious life she'd been blessed with.

But now it was time for some serious shopping.

CHAPTER FOUR

Gateway Promenade was an outdoor mall that Emily had rarely visited. There were several stores in the vicinity that she'd frequented on occasion, one being an eyeglass shop when she'd needed new spectacles.

Most of the women she knew agreed that the majority of stores at this particular mall catered more to teens and young men and women in their twenties and thirties. Emily decided that made it her perfect destination.

When she reached for her purse to call an Uber, it struck her that not only didn't she have a handbag, she didn't have a phone.

A purse, along with a wallet, rose to the top of her must-buy list. Then a prepaid phone that would get her by until she had money coming in, and finally—and this was what she was most excited about—new clothes and shoes.

Though determined not to squander her money, neither would she deny herself the pleasure of the shopping experience. When she'd been young, there had been no money for frivolous purchases. The hotel her father had owned had been struggling, and each dime had been precious.

Thankfully, the dark skies had passed with no more than a

heavy sprinkle. The day was beautiful, and it wasn't much of a walk to the mall. On the way, Emily reveled in her youthful legs, strong and sturdy with no aches or pains.

The Promenade, designed with businesses clustered around a central courtyard, boasted not only leafy trees and an abundance of colorful flowers, but a fountain that doubled as a wishing well.

The fun of perusing the purses in the first store she entered kept Emily busy for a full thirty minutes. She finally settled on what the sales clerk called a hobo bag in a very impractical apricot color.

"This is one of my faves." The girl, who looked about twelve but was undoubtedly older, smiled as she scanned both the purse and matching wallet. "The color is dope."

Thankfully, Emily knew that *dope* meant *lovely*. She smiled and pulled a couple of bills from her tote, laying them on the counter. "I was wondering if you could do me a favor and cut off the tags? I don't plan on returning either item, and I'd like to use them right now."

For the first time, the girl appeared to notice that Emily had pulled the money out of the canvas bag slung over her shoulder.

Seeing the question in her eyes, Emily improvised. "When I looked in my closet, there wasn't a single purse that I could see bringing with me today."

All true, Emily thought, only because there hadn't been a single purse in the room.

"I hear ya." The girl chuckled. "I'm like that, too."

With quick, precise movements, the clerk cut off the tags, put the purse and wallet in a handled sack and handed it to Emily, along with her change.

"Thanks for your help," she told the girl.

"No problem."

Emily was still smiling at the reply that had somehow replaced *you're welcome* as she strode out of the shop and into a big-box anchor store, where she picked up a prepaid smartphone and an Apple Watch.

The directions for activating the phone with three months of talk/text appeared straightforward. Still, since she had no one to call, Emily decided she'd wait until she was back in her room to do the setup.

In time, she would have friends she would want to contact and who would need a way to contact her, but for now she appreciated the anonymity. It gave her time to get her ducks in a row.

A brief stop at a table in the courtyard gave her the chance to put her money and driver's license into the wallet, which she then placed into the purse.

The canvas tote went into the handled shopping bag, along with her new phone. She smiled to herself. Now she was ready for some serious shopping.

Two hours later, Emily returned to the hotel, flushed with the knowledge of a job well done.

She dropped her new purchases off in her room and changed into one of her new outfits. After taking a moment to admire the beauty makeover that she'd had done at a cosmetics counter, she ran her new brush through her hair and headed down the stairs.

Though she could have eaten at the mall, she was in the mood to celebrate the first day of her new life with something different.

Today's early luncheon felt like it had happened eons ago. While the excitement had sustained Emily through her shopping endeavors, all the walking and shopping had stirred her appetite.

Thankfully, the River Walk, with its plethora of restaurants, was only a hop, skip and a jump away. Emily felt a shiver of excitement as she strolled in the early evening air. Music from a band farther down Cripple Creek added to the festive atmosphere.

Emily loved the lights, both white and colored, that businesses strung across outdoor seating areas and around windows.

Even though it wasn't dark yet—*thank you, summer*—the ornate lampposts along the River Walk had already clicked on.

Flags advertising the upcoming Blues, Brews and Barbecue fest fluttered from the posts, the bright orange and yellow colors drawing the eye.

Emily knew all about the annual craft beer festival, or rather, she'd heard about it, but had never attended. Though it was open to any adult twenty-one and over, in her mind the event was geared toward the young.

She glanced down at her puff-sleeve tee, wide-leg trousers in a plant pattern and new strappy sandals. She recalled the image in her hotel room mirror and smiled. Emily had the feeling a Blues, Brews and Barbecue fest was in her future.

At the mall, it seemed as if every woman her age wore sandals with toes painted a variety of vibrant colors. Her changeover hadn't included a pedicure, a fact noticed when she'd been trying on sandals this afternoon.

Yes, a pedicure and a manicure were definitely in her future. She felt a surge of anticipation, then was struck by how odd it was to be planning a trip to a nail salon and deciding which of the many restaurants would get her business tonight when she no longer existed.

For a brief second, the thought had her sobering. Until she remembered she was still very much alive. The body that had been her home for the past ninety-two years had simply been replaced with a newer, sportier model.

The only thing she regretted was bringing pain to those she'd left behind. Once again, she reassured herself that her body had been wearing out and her time would have been up soon enough.

Right now, she was alive and had been given this amazing opportunity. She wasn't going to waste a single moment of it on regret.

∼

After studying the posted menus of several restaurants along the River Walk, Emily went with the "tasting menu" at the Black Apron Bistro. The chef's choices included an appetizer of scallop crudo and a main course of grilled octopus.

The carefully selected wine pairings to complement each course only enhanced the dining experience. Emily found the octopus surprisingly tasty and the Vermentino, a light-bodied white wine, an excellent choice.

When she'd asked the server what was for dessert, Clark, who'd been subtly flirting, winked and told her she was going to love the mignardises.

Unfamiliar with the word, she'd had to ask, and he'd told her they were bite-sized sweet treats. She would receive a plate containing a macaron, a truffle, a petit four and a fruit tartlet. She was offered a digestif or coffee.

As Emily had already consumed enough alcohol throughout the meal—albeit in small portions—she chose the coffee.

Clark's constant attention, despite his other tables filling up, had made her dining experience all the more pleasurable.

When he wasn't seeing to the needs of his other customers, he stood tableside, visiting with her. It was almost, Emily thought, like having a very enjoyable dinner companion.

Unfortunately, as business picked up, Clark's visits to her table became less frequent.

While waiting for him to bring her dessert and coffee, she spotted Chloe and Jaclyn approaching the hostess stand. Emily's heart twisted, knowing that the grief she saw on Chloe's face was for her.

Since Emily had arrived before the rush and all the single tables had been occupied, the hostess had sat her at a four-top in the outdoor dining area.

"I'd be happy to take your name." The hostess's voice carried easily on the still, evening air. "Right now, we're looking at a forty-minute wait."

Jaclyn and Chloe exchanged a look. Chloe gave her head a little shake.

"Thanks anyway." Jaclyn offered the hostess a polite smile. "We'll try another time."

As the two strode by, Emily gestured to the empty chairs at her table and said, "You may join me, if you'd like."

Emily had been taught proper manners from a young age. Calling out to virtual strangers and inviting them to join you at your table simply was not done.

The two women moved to the waist-high ornate fence surrounding the outdoor seating. As they stepped closer, Emily saw recognition dawn on Chloe's face. "You're Emily. Emily Curtis."

"That's right." Emily's heart gave a little lurch. After all those years of closeness, she and Chloe were now strangers.

Chloe turned to Jaclyn. "Emily was the guest I was checking in this afternoon."

Chloe performed a quick introduction, and Emily learned Jaclyn's last name was Edwards and that her father owned the Oasis.

The sadness on Chloe's face had Emily yearning to spring to her feet and enfold the young woman in her arms the way she had when Chloe had been a child.

Good sense had her remaining seated.

Jaclyn shot Emily a look of apology. "Sorry for interrupting your check-in. It was sort of an emergency."

"Chloe and I had finished our business," Emily assured her.

"How do you like your room?" Jaclyn asked, sounding more polite than truly interested.

"It's lovely."

"I'm glad." Jaclyn shifted her gaze to Chloe. "What do you want to do?"

"This works for me," Chloe told her friend, then offered Emily a tentative smile. "We'd love to join you, if you're sure we wouldn't be intruding."

"I'd love the company." The warmth in Emily's voice appeared to seal the deal. At least for Chloe.

Jaclyn hesitated for only a second more. "I'll grab menus from the hostess."

The two women were just getting seated when Clark appeared with Emily's dessert plate and coffee.

Chloe's amber eyes widened. "Those look amazing."

"Have one. Or two." Emily nudged the plate in Chloe's direction, then turned to Jaclyn. "Please, help yourself."

"None for me." Jaclyn lifted a staying hand, then added as more of an afterthought, "Thanks, though."

"They look incredible." Chloe heaved a sigh filled with regret. "I should probably eat some real food first."

Jaclyn turned to Chloe. "Are you going with the blueberry bison burger with roasted vegetables?"

Chloe chuckled. "You know me so well."

"Make that two." Jaclyn smiled up at Clark.

Clark inclined his head. "Anything to drink?"

Once he'd taken their drink orders, Clark swept up the menus, his gaze lingering on Emily. "It shouldn't be long. The kitchen is on fire tonight."

"Hopefully, he means that figuratively," Emily quipped.

Jaclyn's brows pulled together.

Chloe laughed.

"You both already knew what you wanted," Emily observed, glancing from one woman to the other. "You really didn't need menus."

Jaclyn shrugged. "We thought we might."

"When the blueberry bison burgers are on the menu, that's what we usually get." Chloe glanced at Emily. "What did you have?"

"I went with the tasting menu." Emily gave them a quick course-by-course rundown.

Chloe wrinkled her nose. "I tried octopus once. Now, it may have been how it was prepared, but it seemed rubbery, and I didn't care for the taste. But you liked yours, right?"

"It was incredible." Emily gave a little laugh. "I was tempted to go with the seared scallops, a personal favorite, but that would have been the safe choice. I was feeling adventurous tonight."

"That's a lot of food," Jaclyn commented, then glanced at Chloe. "I could never eat that much."

"It was a lot," Emily admitted. "But everything was amazing, and I ate it all."

Jaclyn offered a grudging nod. "It's good to tap into our adventurous side."

"I'm trying to stretch myself." Emily leaned forward. "Abraham Maslow once said, 'In any given moment, we have two options—to step forward into growth or to step back into safety.' I've gone the safe route one too many times."

Emily hadn't even finished speaking when tears filled Chloe's eyes and slipped down her cheeks.

Emily resisted the urge to reach out and ask what was wrong, the way she had when Chloe had been young.

Blinking rapidly and appearing embarrassed by the show of emotion, Chloe hurriedly brushed away the tears. "Sorry. I had a friend who loved that quote."

"It's okay, Chloe." Jaclyn's voice was as soft as the hand she placed on her friend's arm. She turned to Emily and explained, "She lost someone very close to her today."

"Til, that was her name, well, actually it was Matilda, but she went by Til." Chloe sniffled, then pulled a tissue from her purse. "She was found dead in a park this afternoon."

"Oh no." Emily forced surprise into her voice. "What happened?"

"She was really old," Jaclyn pointed out. "Like, ancient."

Chloe shot Jaclyn a glinting glance before refocusing on Emily. "She was ninety-two, but a young ninety-two, if you know what I mean."

"I do." Emily offered a sympathetic smile. "Was this woman a relative?"

Chloe shook her head and appeared to steady. She took a sip of her cola. "Not by blood, but she was like a grandma to me. My parents traveled a lot for their business when I was young. They hired Til to watch me when they were gone. It felt as if I was with her more than with my parents growing up. I-I loved her."

Emily's heart twisted.

"The thing I regret the most," Chloe continued without any prompting, not appearing to notice when the server placed the plate of burger and vegetables before her, "is that I didn't spend more time with her when I first got back to GraceTown. Now, it's too late."

"I'm sure she understood." Again, Emily had to resist the urge to reach over and give Chloe's hand a squeeze.

"I don't know, maybe, I hope." Chloe expelled a heavy sigh and picked up her fork.

"You've only been back a few months," Jaclyn reminded her. "You were busy getting settled."

"I should have made time for what was important," Chloe insisted. "Think of your own grandmother. She won't be around forever."

Jaclyn rolled her eyes. "Don't get going on her."

Sensing a sore subject, Emily steered the conversation back to Chloe. "Where were you before you returned to GraceTown?"

Emily took a sip of coffee and nibbled on a petit four. She, of course, already knew the answer, but the more Chloe spoke, the more she appeared to steady.

"I went away to college. First to get my bachelor's, then I picked up a master's, because, hey, why not?" Chloe gave a laugh.

"You always were an overachiever." Jaclyn's tone held a teasing edge.

Chloe laughed. "I guess."

"What did you get your degrees in?" Emily asked, wanting to keep the conversation going.

"Liberal arts and hospitality management." Chloe shook her head. "Not exactly the most marketable of concentrations, but it's what I like. After graduation, I worked in the hospitality industry in Miami. Then, well, things went south, and I came back here. Jaclyn and I were roommates at Cornell and kept in touch. Thanks to her recommendation, her father offered me a job managing the Oasis."

"You'd have gotten the job without me," Jaclyn insisted. "Your résumé speaks for itself. He was lucky to get someone with your qualifications."

Emily agreed. Any employer would be lucky to have Chloe. "What about you, Jaclyn? Do you also work at the Oasis?"

"I don't." Jaclyn stabbed a roasted carrot. "I love my dad and all, but us working together, well, there is such a thing as being too close. I'm the assistant catering manager at the Grand Manse."

The Grand Manse had once been a private residence. Located on twenty acres, it now housed the former owner's extensive art collection. The house and land had been bequeathed to the city with the stipulation that the home and gardens be used for special events that would enrich the lives of GraceTown residents.

Emily had known Birdie Hollowell, the former owner. Though they hadn't been close, she admired Birdie's philanthropic nature and all she'd done for the town they both loved.

"I didn't realize the Manse did outside catering." The words slipped out before Emily could remind herself that she was supposed to be new to GraceTown.

"Until recently, we only catered on-site events. But it made sense to take on outside events to bolster revenue." The first genuine smile that Emily had seen since Jaclyn had sat down lifted her lips. "I'm jazzed about the changes."

"Jaclyn is the one dealing with the outside venues and clients." Chloe beamed at her friend. "You're the perfect person for the job."

"Thanks, Chloe." Jaclyn shifted her focus to Emily. "What is it you do, Emily?"

Emily's hand stilled on the cup she'd just brought to her lips. She lowered it back to the saucer without taking a drink.

Her mind raced as she fought to recall what she'd read on the résumé Serena had provided. The résumé she had only skimmed.

Concert violinist.

Dear God, couldn't Serena have picked something more normal? Then Emily reminded herself there was nothing normal about any of this.

"I received a bachelor of music degree from Juilliard. My instrument of choice is the violin." Under the table, Emily wiped suddenly sweaty hands against her napkin.

"Juilliard." Admiration shone in Chloe's amber depths.

"That's cool." Jaclyn took a bite of her bison burger, her gaze turning sharp and assessing.

Emily hoped the questioning would end there. She opened her mouth, ready to steer the conversation in another direction, but she didn't get the chance when Jaclyn spoke first.

"What have you done since graduation?"

"Most recently, I played for the Baltimore Symphony Orchestra." That had been the last position on the résumé. Emily was almost sure of it.

For over a century, the Baltimore Symphony Orchestra had been recognized as one of the leading organizations in the country. She wondered if its close proximity to GraceTown was why Serena had made the orchestra part of her history.

Emily's plan was to go through the paperwork Serena had

included once she returned to her hotel room later tonight. If Emily had done it earlier, she'd have been prepared for these types of questions.

"Why did you leave?" Chloe asked the question that Emily had hoped neither of them would raise.

"I was ready for a change." Though Emily had no idea why a concert violinist was the background she'd been given, drinking the youth elixir had been about change. "Though I have to wonder if that was a smart move."

The questioning looks in the eyes of the two women had Emily explaining. "I don't have another position lined up."

Jaclyn arched a brow. "You came to GraceTown. There's no symphony here."

"I realize that." Emily took another drink of coffee. "I'm not looking to go back to a symphony."

The questioning look in Jaclyn's eyes had Emily continuing. "I've got a few ideas, some possibilities, none I'm ready to share."

"I respect that." Chloe wiped blueberry sauce off her lips with the edge of her napkin. "I have to admit, though, like Jaclyn, I'm curious. Why GraceTown? Do you have family here?"

No way was Emily making something up. She knew from a lifetime of living here that, while there might be six degrees of separation in most situations, in GraceTown it was down to three.

"No family. Or friends." Once again, Emily brought the coffee cup to her lips, the action giving her time to think. "I heard GraceTown is like Sedona. You know, a place where one can tap into the frequencies of the universe. I was intrigued."

"Frequencies of the universe?" Jaclyn's brows pulled together. "What does that mean? I've never heard that term."

"I have." Chloe lifted a hand, like a schoolgirl in a classroom. "Til had a friend who lived in Sedona. She visited once when Til was watching me. The week Vicki was here, I heard that phrase a lot."

"But what does it mean?" Jaclyn asked, puzzlement filling her blue eyes.

Emily hoped Chloe would explain, but Chloe only stared expectantly at her.

It had been so long since she and Vicki had talked that Emily fought to recall what she'd said. "It's all about an area having a unique energy, places where the earth's energy is amplified and heightened."

"I grew up here. Some people believe in unexplainable happenings, but I've never known anyone who experienced anything the least bit strange. Personally, I think it's all a joke." Jaclyn's expression seemed to indicate that anyone who believed differently was a fool.

"I'm not sure what I think." Chloe shrugged as her gaze returned to Emily. "Though I do believe GraceTown has a good vibe."

As much as Emily enjoyed spending time with Chloe, she was finding this discussion and all the questions a bit too much.

"A very good vibe," Emily agreed, pushing her chair back and standing. She dropped several bills on the table. "I hate to rush off, but I have a date."

The fact that the two didn't ask any questions or offer much of a protest told Emily that, tonight, three had definitely been a crowd.

CHAPTER FIVE

Okay, so her date hadn't been firmed up, and it was with a bike, not a man, but still...

On her way to the Black Apron, Emily had walked by a business that was either new or somehow had previously escaped her notice.

Gear Up & Go Bike Shop was a bike rental, sales and repair business. From the number of riders inside, it appeared to do a brisk business.

Decades ago, Til had ridden her bike daily all over Grace-Town. The year she turned seventy-five, she'd sold her Schwinn after falling and banging up both herself and the bike.

Though she hadn't broken anything on that long-ago day when she'd hit a rock with her front tire and lost control, she had been badly bruised. Worse, her confidence had been shattered.

Excitement now tripped through her veins. This pretty silver bicycle was all hers, at least for the next two hours. That should give her more than enough time for a leisurely ride to the Dairy Sweet across town and back.

While Emily might have been full when she'd left the bistro, to her way of thinking, there was always room for ice cream.

She walked the Trek to the bike lane. Holding her breath, Emily got on and began to pedal. Her breath came out in a joyous whoosh as she discovered that riding a bike really was something you never forgot.

Reveling in the feel of the bike smoothly gliding over the path, the wind caressing her cheeks, Emily was filled with a sense of wonder.

How long had it been since she'd ridden so effortlessly?

By the time she reached the ice cream shop known for its peach soft serve, she wasn't even out of breath.

The sun shone warm on her face as she stood in line with families, couples and other singles.

Once Emily had her cone, she took a seat on one of the white lacquered benches and savored the creamy peach taste. Closing her eyes for a second, she embraced the moment.

"Is it that good?"

Emily opened her eyes to find a man with hair as blond as hers standing by the bench. She smiled. "It really is."

"I haven't seen you around here before."

Emily gestured with her head toward his cone. "Vanilla?"

He offered a sheepish smile. "Boring and predictable. What can I say?"

Chuckling, Emily smiled. "I sincerely doubt that."

The man not only looked hot in his shorts and shirt, he possessed a confidence that had him approaching her, a woman he didn't know.

He gestured. "Mind if I sit?"

Emily glanced down and realized she sat smack-dab in the middle of the bench. She scooted over. "Not at all."

He returned her smile as he dropped down beside her. "Josh Ferrell."

"Emily Curtis."

He studied her as he licked his cone, then nodded. "The name suits you."

Her lips curved as her tongue swirled around the ice cream. "It was a good choice."

"Sometimes parents really do know best," Josh agreed.

They finished off their cones as the sun began to dip. Emily had to remind herself only once to temper her words lest she give away her true age.

Josh, who she learned was in mortgage lending at First Grace-Town Bank, brought up the recession of the late 1970s, early 1980s. Emily nearly mentioned she had a friend who'd gotten a mortgage in 1981 with an interest rate of eighteen percent.

Thankfully, she'd been smart enough to keep the memory to herself. Besides, there was plenty else to talk about. She found herself enjoying the conversation so much she didn't pay attention to the alarm sounding.

"Is that your phone?" Josh paused in the story he was telling.

Emily blinked, then realized that setting the chimes sound as her alarm had been a mistake. It might have captured his attention, but it hadn't hers. She abruptly stood. "I need to go."

Though twenty minutes should be enough time to get the bike back on time, she didn't want to be late and risk having to pay a late fee.

Josh pushed to his feet. "Right now?"

The disappointment in his eyes told her he'd been enjoying the conversation as much as she had. How long had it been, Emily wondered, since she'd had a lengthy conversation with a man who wasn't someone's husband? "It was lovely meeting you."

His gaze remained fixed on her. "I enjoyed our conversation. Maybe we can—"

The chimes sounded again—her backup alarm kicking in.

"I'm sure our paths will cross again." She brushed a casual kiss across his cheek, surprised at how natural it seemed. "Thanks for keeping me company, Josh."

Climbing onto her bike, she headed toward Gear Up & Go, unable to keep from smiling.

After returning the bike, she made a quick stop at Sip and Charm Spirits to pick up a bottle of wine. Then Emily returned to her room, her head spinning and her spirits high. When she'd awakened this morning, she'd anticipated having a regular day. Nothing special. Nothing out of the ordinary. Lunch and cards with friends, starting to read a new novel and perhaps spending an hour working in her garden.

Instead, her world had gone topsy-turvy. Matilda Beemis was gone, replaced by Emily Curtis, a violin virtuoso.

She eyed the violin case on top of the dresser. If she picked it up, would she even know how to play it? Another unknown.

Right now, she had other priorities.

After turning on the water in the tub, Emily began to strip. When the claw-foot tub was nearly full, she tossed in the lavender-scented bath bomb she'd picked up earlier today.

While waiting for it to dissolve, she put her hair in the satin bonnet that had been another of her afternoon purchases. The young woman who'd rung it up had told her that her grandmother loved this style. Emily had only smiled.

She uncorked the bottle of wine and poured some into one of the glasses she'd bought, then set her book beside the glass of wine and the tub.

Realizing there was a step she'd nearly forgotten, Emily hurriedly grabbed the chamomile bubble bar and placed it under the running water. Out of the corner of her eye, she caught sight of her body in the mirror as she bent over.

The supple, toned skin and soft, gentle curves had her staring in disbelief. Though nothing had changed on the inside, everything was different on the outside.

The wisdom of experience and the vigor of youth. Normally, you had one, but not the other. Serena had been right. This was a gift.

Smiling, Emily turned off the faucets, then lowered herself

into the warm water of the deep tub, confident that when it came time to get out, she would do so with ease.

Just one more thing to love about the new her.

Emily awoke the next morning, ready to seize the day with both hands. She wasn't sure exactly what was on tap for today, but whatever it was, it wouldn't involve food or sitting around. She was determined to find an activity that had been out of her reach as a ninety-two-year-old woman.

Her gaze drifted to the instrument case she had yet to open. Soon, very soon, she was going to take out the violin and see if she could play. But not now.

Before she dressed, she used her phone to search for fun activities and had found just the thing. If she hadn't seen the advertisement on the town's website, the thought of climbing a rock wall wouldn't have entered her mind.

Now, dressed in stretchy shorts, a fitted tee and sneakers, her entire body thrummed with excitement. Though she knew absolutely nothing about how to climb a rock wall, she was ready and eager to learn.

Emily glanced toward the reception area when she reached the hotel's main level, disappointed not to see Chloe behind the desk. Studying her résumé last night had left her feeling confident that she could now answer any and all questions tossed her way.

Emily had hoped that if Chloe were working, there would be time for them to chat for a few. While spending time with her and Jaclyn at the Black Apron had been enjoyable, she had definitely felt like the outsider.

She could only hope that when she returned, Chloe would be at the desk.

. . .

Reaching the sidewalk, Emily found herself wishing for the bike she'd turned in last night. For a second, she was tempted to rent another, but Vertical Ascent wasn't so far that she couldn't walk or—and this thought had her smiling—jog there.

After taking a second to stretch, Emily took off at a light jog. The rhythmic slap of her shoes against the pavement brought a smile to her lips. It was early enough that the sidewalks were clear of all the foot traffic that would have made taking this route impossible.

The building housing Vertical Ascent soared high, the modern design, with its steeply pointed roof and glass and chrome exterior, fit the business to perfection.

The level of noise inside surprised her, until she realized that Vertical Ascent shared the building with Urban Movement, a family-friendly indoor adventure and trampoline park.

If the noise coming from that side of the building was any indication, the business was doing well.

Ignoring the Urban Movement check-in desk, Emily strode over to the one sporting a VA logo. A college-age girl with a name tag proclaiming her to be Kayla smiled a welcome.

"I'd like to try the rock-climbing wall," Emily told her. "I'm not sure what that all involves, but that's why I'm here."

For just a second, the girl's blond brows pulled together.

"Is that a problem?" Emily hadn't seen anything about making an appointment, but maybe—

"Not a problem," Kayla said hastily. "It's just that we have a group here from Funds Hub. They're here for a team-building afternoon."

"Funds Hub, the company that designs mobile banking software?"

"You've heard of it?"

Emily nearly said a church friend's great-grandson had started the company, but she settled for a nod.

"We have a limited number of staff, as they brought more

employees than we were expecting, but that's great," Kayla quickly added, then picked up a phone and held up a finger. "I just need to make sure we have someone to help you."

After a brief conversation, she smiled brightly. "Chuck is available. He'll be here shortly. While we're waiting for him, since this is your first visit, I'll need you to fill out and sign a waiver."

Emily finished the paperwork right before Chuck appeared. Tall and muscular with a shaved head and serious brown eyes, he nodded approvingly at her hair, tied back with a band that Kayla had provided.

"I've never done this before," Emily told Chuck as he walked with her toward several rock-climbing walls.

"Normally, we offer orientation sessions, but since we have a group here—"

"Funds Hub."

"Yes, since they're here and we have limited space for others, I'm going to give you a one-on-one orientation."

Emily offered him a smile. "I appreciate that."

She listened intently as he took her on a short tour, talking about the gym's layout, safety procedures and basic climbing techniques.

Once Emily rented climbing shoes, a harness and a chalk bag, Chuck made sure everything fit her properly. He then had her practice falling and landing on her feet with slightly bent knees.

Emily found it great fun.

"You're doing great." Chuck nodded approvingly.

Emily felt her confidence surge. She liked the idea that climbing not only had lots of physical benefits, but that it required her using problem-solving skills and mental focus.

The Funds Hub people appeared concentrated around the more difficult routes. Chuck took her to one marked with a green dot.

"This is a route for beginners like yourself. It has larger holds and is designed for someone who hasn't climbed before."

Emily's gaze slid to the wall marked with a black dot, where many of the Funds Hubbers stood, laughing and talking while waiting their turn.

"Don't worry about anyone else. This is about you. Take your time and climb at a pace that feels comfortable for you."

Emily only nodded. No need to tell him that she wasn't wishing for a more difficult course. It was the camaraderie she envied.

She missed having friends with her, cheering her on and offering encouragement, with her doing the same for them.

That would come in time, Emily assured herself. Right now, she had a wall to conquer.

CHAPTER SIX

On the way back to the hotel, flushed from several successful climbs, Emily decided she might as well add a yoga class to her day's accomplishments.

Soon after moving back to GraceTown, Chloe had raved about discovering Vital Yoga. Emily recalled thinking at the time that the recently opened business must be pretty special to provoke such accolades.

Emily had never set foot in a yoga class. Though yoga had been around for thousands of years, she didn't recall it being "a thing" until the 1960s.

While enjoying a protein smoothie at GraceTown Juice, Emily pulled up the studio's website on her phone and found the class times.

It still surprised her how easy it had been to set up her phone and watch. She had considered herself to be relatively computer savvy for a ninety-two-year-old, but her new body appeared to have been blessed with mad tech skills.

Finishing off the smoothie, she glanced at her new watch and smiled. If she hurried, she'd have just enough time to make the next class.

When Emily stepped into Vital Yoga thirty minutes later, the studio's welcoming feel began with the tall woman at the door.

The woman, her body lean and muscular, wore a midriff-baring tank top and yoga pants. Curly dark hair, styled in what Emily recognized as double Dutch box braids, suited her strikingly beautiful face.

"Welcome to Vital Yoga. I'm Tibby Washington." She offered a friendly smile. "How may I help you?"

"Hi, I'm Emily Curtis." Emily glanced around this outer area of the studio that appeared to sell everything from vitamins and supplements to cute pants and tops. "I thought I'd take in a class. Though I have to warn you, I've never done yoga before and don't have a clue what to do."

"No worries. The classes here are for all levels. I'm the instructor today. I'll be offering guidance throughout the practice to you and the other students."

"Any feedback will be appreciated." Emily wondered if she would find the poses easy or difficult. She had so much to learn about her new body.

"If you have any questions, don't hesitate to ask."

"I do have a quick one. Who do I pay for the class?"

"This first one is free." Tibby stepped back from the door, allowing other students to enter. "After that, it's up to you. Some prefer to pay class by class, although buying ten sessions or paying by the month ends up being the most cost-effective options."

"I don't know…" Emily tapped two fingers against her lips.

"Take the class. See what you think. No need to decide now." Tibby gestured. "There's a sheet on the table over there detailing the various pricing options. The information is also on the website."

"Thanks." As students continued to stream through the door, Emily noticed most had mats tucked under their arms.

She turned back to Tibby. "I didn't bring a mat."

The instructor offered a reassuring smile. "We have some at the back of the studio. While some students prefer to bring their own, it isn't necessary."

"Great."

"Also," Tibby gestured to the tiny purse Emily had brought with her and then to her shoes, "we have shoe trays and shelves at the back of the room where you can store your bag and shoes. I encourage you to bring only essentials into the practice area. We like to maintain a clutter-free and calming environment."

"So much to learn," Emily murmured. She wasn't complaining, simply thinking of all she was now free to experience.

"Class will start in a few minutes." Tibby smiled and greeted several students, then turned back to Emily. "As I said, you'll find mats at the back of the studio. Grab one and set it wherever you feel comfortable."

"Thanks, Ms. Washington—"

"Please, call me Tibby." The woman smiled. "We're not overly formal here."

"Well, Tibby," Emily smiled, "I think this is going to be quite an adventure."

"Seriously, any questions, let me know."

Emily nodded, but knew she wouldn't disrupt the session with a bunch of newbie questions. Inside the studio, she noticed most seemed to prefer the front or the middle of the room.

Settling the mat in what she hoped was the back row, Emily felt her heart rate quicken. She could do this. She had youth and vigor and desire.

If she liked it, she would come back and learn more. If she didn't, she'd find another new activity to explore. The thought of the endless possibilities had blood racing through her veins.

Three minutes before the class was scheduled to start, two men strolled in. Both wore athletic shorts and T-shirts. The blond one appeared to know what to do, grabbing a mat, then motioning to his friend to do the same.

It took Emily a second to make the connection. The blond man was Joe Wexman. Folklore studies professor at Collister. Married to Sophie, great-granddaughter of Beulah Jessup—now deceased—a classmate of Til's.

In high school, long, long ago, her closest friends had been Beulah and Irene Anderson. After Irene's passing, she and Beulah had grown even closer.

All her classmates were gone now. She'd been the last woman standing.

The men set their mats beside Emily, making a row of the three of them. She offered the two a smile, then turned her gaze to the front and gave Tibby her full attention.

The soft instrumental music filling the studio relaxed and soothed. When Tibby began speaking, Emily found her voice as calming as the music.

"Namaste, everyone." Tibby glanced around the class. "I'm very glad to see all of you. I invite you to set an intention for your practice today. During the session, focus on something specific you wish to bring into your life. This could be peace, gratitude or anything personally meaningful."

Emily considered what should be her focus. Gratitude, she decided, for being given this opportunity to experience life in a new and different way.

"We'll begin with a brief centering exercise."

The dark-haired guy, the one closest to her, murmured something to his friend that Emily couldn't make out.

Joe kept his attention firmly fixed on Tibby even as his lips quirked upward.

"Please find a comfortable seated position on your mat, either cross-legged, kneeling or sitting on a bolster or block for support." Tibby's soft tone was as smooth as melted butter.

Emily chose the cross-legged pose. Out of the corner of her eye, she noticed both men following her lead.

"Now, gently close your eyes."

Everything around Emily faded except for Tibby and her voice.

As the session progressed, Emily continued to follow Tibby's directions to the best of her ability. Sometimes she hit the mark and found the pose relatively easy to master. Other times, she fell far short.

"May I show you how to deepen that stretch ever so slightly?"

Startled, Emily looked up into Tibby's dark eyes. "Please."

"Proper alignment is essential. Since you have that, this is a way to deepen the stretch."

Emily followed Tibby's instructions and immediately felt the difference. She glanced at Tibby and smiled. "Thank you."

"You're very welcome." Tibby moved on to Joe.

"Joe, for Warrior II, you need to ensure your front knee is directly above your ankle, and it tracks in line with your second toe."

Tibby then turned her attention to the dark-haired guy. "Keep your arms parallel to the ground. Good. That's good. Now find stability in your stance by pressing the outer edge of your back foot firmly into the mat. Yes, just like that."

As if satisfied, Tibby moved on.

The hour went by quickly, concluding with Tibby leading the class through a series of cool-down poses, culminating with a Corpse pose. Emily thought this one especially appropriate, considering what had recently happened to her.

As she lay on the mat, her arms and legs comfortably apart, palms facing up and eyes closed, Emily found herself letting go of any remaining tension.

The final breathing exercise, involving deep inhales and exhales, brought the class to a close.

"Thank you for your practice and dedication. I encourage you to carry the benefits of your practice with you into your daily life." Tibby brought her palms together and bowed her head. "Namaste."

"Namaste," the class echoed.

Reaching down to pick up her mat, Emily couldn't help but smile. Yoga definitely had a place in her new life.

"How did you enjoy the class?"

Emily already had her shoes on and bag over her shoulder when Tibby approached her.

"I loved it. I would have told you, but you were busy with other students." Emily glanced at her watch. "I don't have time now, but I'll definitely be looking to purchase a package of ten sessions to start."

"Fabulous. Keep in mind we also have monthly rates that are even more affordable."

While Emily knew that she wanted to return and knew she could come again next week, after that she didn't know what she'd be doing.

Endless possibilities.

The world was, as her good friend Irene Anderson used to say, her oyster.

"I'm always available to answer any questions you might have." The warmth in Tibby's eyes was reflected in her voice. "I hope to see you back very soon."

Emily had turned toward the door when she heard Tibby greet Joe Wexman.

"Joe, it's good to see you again. And you brought a friend."

"I lost a bet."

Emily recognized that voice as belonging to the dark-haired guy.

Tibby laughed. "Well, I hope you enjoyed yourself anyway."

"Joe tells me I need to chill." The man chuckled. "He's probably right."

Emily was out the door before she could hear Tibby's

response. Once on the sidewalk, she turned in the direction of the River Walk.

Near the entrance, a twentysomething woman played a keyboard and sang. A portable amplification system did a nice job of projecting her voice while a video setup recorded.

The emotional song, with its powerful melody and heartfelt lyrics, clearly captivated the small audience that stood nearby.

Emily understood. The lyrics, about being true to yourself, were something everyone could relate to.

In her head, Emily imagined how a violin would add to the listener's enjoyment. As the last note of the song ended, Emily not only clapped with the rest of the crowd, she reached into her bag, pulled out a ten-dollar bill and dropped it into the hat.

For a second, her eyes met those of the girl with the mass of curly brown hair, and something passed between them—musician to musician.

Musician? Seriously, where had that thought even come from? Yet, as Emily stood there, her fingers itched to pick up the violin and give life to the sweet music running through her head.

She suddenly wanted nothing more than to go to her hotel room, take the violin out of its case and play.

Something, maybe it was that stirring deep inside her soul, said that it was time.

Turning on her heel, Emily headed in the direction of the hotel and her instrument.

Once in her room, Emily focused on the case atop the dresser. Ready to embrace possibilities, she opened it. Her breath caught at the luxurious velvet interior and the glossy instrument nestled in the purple softness.

Without thought, as if she'd performed the action a thousand times before, she lifted a shoulder pad out of the case and attached it to the back of the instrument.

Then she applied rosin to the bow hair, somehow knowing that the sticky material was what helped the strings to vibrate and produce sound. Emily wasn't sure how she knew this step was necessary any more than she knew—just *knew*—that she could play this instrument.

This was her opportunity, Emily thought, to see if that intuition held true. She was on the top floor of the hotel, and most everyone staying here were likely out of their rooms at this time of day. If she played softly, she shouldn't disturb anyone still around.

There was sheet music in the case, but Emily didn't take it out. Instead, she closed her eyes and began with the tune the girl on the street had been playing yesterday.

The sweet sounds emanating from the instrument touched something deep inside her. By the time she finished, Emily had to blink away tears.

At that moment, she realized that Serena had not only given her the gift of youth, she'd given her the gift of music. Had that been deliberate?

Emily found herself seized with a sudden desire, a need to play more, but she knew this wasn't the place for that.

Packing up the violin, Emily slung the case over her back and decided to see what playing on the street was like.

Just one more new adventure on a day filled with them.

The River Walk was so close that Emily reached the entrance in a matter of minutes. The girl with the gorgeous voice was still there.

At the sound of Emily's footsteps, the girl stopped what she was doing and turned. "Something I can help you with?"

Emily lifted the case. "I wondered if we could play a few songs together?"

The girl didn't hesitate. She immediately shook her head. "I work alone."

"I heard you play. You're good."

"Thanks, but as I said, I—"

"I'm good, too. My instrument would add, not take away."

"Look." The girl met Emily's gaze head on. "I'm not interested. I'm a solo act, and this is my spot. You need to find your own."

"I don't want to compete with you," Emily assured her. "I just want to—"

"Like I said, not interested." With that comment, the girl turned back to the camera setup.

Emily considered her options. She could walk back to the hotel, but why? Surely there were dozens of places where she could play and enjoy the gorgeous sunshine.

Her lips slowly lifted. She knew the perfect spot.

In the shadow of the Angel of GraceTown, Emily slipped the violin from its case. Anticipation coursed through her veins like an awakened river. Emily wasn't sure what melodies would call to her once she began to play. There were so many clamoring inside her head right now it seemed impossible to just pick one.

Under the benevolent smile of the statue, Emily began to play. She didn't have an amplification system or any backing tracks, though she could see both in her future. Today, it was simply her, a violin and a world of life's experiences.

She thought about Papa and what losing him had been like. The mournful tune that rose up and spilled out had those passing by stopping to listen.

She thought of the friends who were no longer with her. She remembered Vincent.

Emily wrung every bit of emotion out of "Danny Boy" with her bow, her heart swelling and expanding with the music. By the time she finished, her eyes were damp.

She wasn't alone. Several in the audience that had gathered also wiped away tears.

Emily lightened up on the next rendition, playing an acoustic version of an Adele hit, one that Chloe had particularly loved during her teen years, then going folksy with a melody that had people swaying where they stood.

She hadn't left her case open, so she was surprised when men and women came up and placed bills and coins on top of the case, along with sharing smiles and words of thanks with her.

Emily played for what felt like hours, until the tangled emotions inside her quieted and a sense of peace stole over her.

The crowd thinned as dinnertime approached. Emily couldn't believe how much money people had left for her. She smiled as she packed up and considered the endless food options nearby. But when she began walking, instead of strolling to the River Walk and its plethora of eateries, she found herself heading in the direction of her house. Or rather, Til's house.

Knowing her body had been found in the park had her wondering what had been happening since. Would there be an investigation? A funeral? She had a plot next to her parents in the GraceTown cemetery, but had always told friends that when she passed, she didn't want any fuss.

Would they honor her request?

When she reached the block where her house sat, she noticed several cars parked out front. One she recognized as belonging to Beverly and Geraldine.

Emily spotted them on the porch. Though she couldn't be positive, because their bodies blocked her view, it appeared Lisa and Rosemary were with them.

The four women stood, arms wrapped around one another, heads bowed and shoulders shaking. Emily realized they were crying, grieving for her.

For a second, a longing rose up in her, a yearning to go back to the way things had been. These were her friends, women she'd trusted with her life.

When she'd drunk the liquid, she had done it hoping she would be able to rekindle her friendship with them eventually, only in a different way.

That was still possible, she assured herself. She simply had to find a way to reconnect. Finding solace in the possibility, she turned and began walking away from her old home and toward her future.

CHAPTER SEVEN

When Saturday rolled around, Emily realized that this marked her first weekend living at the Oasis. Though she'd experienced much these past five days, she was growing weary of doing all the fun activities alone.

Botton line, she missed talking to her friends.

Yesterday, when she'd gone to Sparkle Nails for a mani-pedi, it had been with the hope of enjoying some casual, even if superficial, conversations. But the women on both sides of her had been engrossed in their phones, and her nail tech talked nonstop about some dumb thing her boyfriend had done.

Emily had never been one for constant chatter, but it was beginning to feel as if she had this new wonderful life and no one to share it with.

Give it time, she told herself as she biked to Culler Lake for what was billed as Lakeside Surge Splash, a full day of fun in the sun.

There were loads of activities for young adults. Unfortunately, Emily arrived late, and the rosters for the volleyball and softball teams were already full.

After watching bits of both games, Emily wandered the area.

Despite knowing she needed to watch her pennies, she rented a paddleboard. It was something she could do alone. Besides, it looked like fun.

Thankfully, she had worn her new swim shorts—navy with white polka dots—and a tank top. The bright pink on her fingers kept drawing her eye, and she couldn't keep from smiling.

She pulled her attention back to the attendant, relieved to hear that the board and paddle came with a life jacket.

Emily could see he was busy. After making sure he'd selected the right equipment for her, he strode off to the next person, a tall redhead who was turning in her board.

"Hey, you need help?"

The redhead was striding toward her.

"I don't even know how to get started." Emily gave a little laugh that managed to sound quite pathetic. She gestured with her head. "The attendants are all so busy…"

"I think they were unprepared for the amount of interest in today's event. I'm Mackenna, by the way."

"Emily."

Mackenna eyed her equipment and gave an approving nod. "Looks like you've got everything you need. Now, pick up the board, fin facing up, and we'll take it over there where the water is calm and relatively shallow."

"You don't have to help me—"

"If not me, then who?"

It was what Emily had said whenever someone had asked why she volunteered to teach literacy, especially to detention center inmates.

"Well, thank you."

"You're welcome." Mackenna stopped and pointed. "Now, place the board in the water. We don't want the fin hitting the bottom, which I don't think it will here."

Following the instructions, Emily not only put the board in

the water, she mounted the board and eventually was steady enough to stand.

"Now, hold the paddle with one hand on the T-grip and the other on the shaft."

Once Emily did as instructed, Mackenna taught her the basic paddling strokes and how to switch sides when paddling for better balance.

"That's good. You're a natural." Mackenna's praise bolstered Emily's confidence. "Remember to distribute your weight evenly on both feet. No, no, don't look down. Look at the horizon. That will help you maintain your balance. Good, that's good."

After more pointers on how to turn the board and dealing with falls, Mackenna pronounced her ready to head to open water.

"Thank you, sincerely."

"You're very welcome." Mackenna studied her for several long seconds. "Have we met before? I feel as if we've met before. Maybe at Destiny? I'm there most Saturday nights."

Emily knew about the popular club where the younger crowd went to drink and dance, but she had never been inside. "I don't think so. But if I see you there, I'll buy you a drink."

Mackenna grinned. "You've got yourself a deal."

It was time to paddle away, but Emily was enjoying this time too much to rush off. She wondered if it would be too pushy to ask if Mackenna had lunch plans. Maybe instead of a drink, they could meet up after Emily turned in her board, and she could buy lunch?

"Hannah." Mackenna waved her arm wildly, then turned back to Emily. "I've got to go. I'll see you around."

"Thanks—" There was no time to say more, as Mackenna was striding over to where her friend stood.

Emily realized with a shock that Mackenna's friend was Lisa's daughter-in-law.

What a small world, Emily thought, then dipped her paddle in the water. With several short, controlled strokes, Emily moved the board forward.

An hour later, Emily turned in the paddleboard. While she was tired, the sense of accomplishment and feeling of relaxation stayed with her long after her feet hit dry land.

Paddleboarding was something she could definitely see doing again. Once she'd turned in her equipment to the still-harried attendant, she was reminded by the growling of her stomach that it was lunchtime.

She could see now that the man running the SUP station had brought a picnic lunch. That thought had never crossed Emily's mind. Though several food trucks were parked nearby, Emily couldn't muster any enthusiasm for their offerings.

Recalling Cuppa Joe was running a $2 pizza slice special today made the decision easy to return to town and grab a bite to eat there.

With her money stash dwindling by the day, Emily realized that sooner—rather than later—she would need to find a more economical place to stay than the hotel. Specifically, someplace she could prepare her own meals. And she should start looking for a job.

The sweet scent of summer hung heavy in the afternoon air as she took the bike path back to town. One thing she would never get tired of, or take for granted, was having strong legs and endless endurance.

The first thing Emily did when she reached the business district was to roll the bicycle into Gear Up & Go. "Here it is, home safe and sound."

Tyler, who had rented the bike to her, turned. He was a lanky young man with a mass of brown hair.

"Always on time." Taking the handlebars, he smiled and studied her. "I mentioned it before, but we've got bikes on sale right now. If you don't mind used, I've got one I could give you a good deal on."

"Which one is it?" Emily glanced around the shop.

He patted the handlebars of the bike she'd just returned. "This beauty."

"How much?"

Though Emily would love having a car, she couldn't afford one. But, depending on price, she might be able to afford a bicycle. Renting one every time she needed transportation was getting expensive.

"I can give it to you for…" Tyler rubbed his chin in thought.

The amount he named seemed fair, but would still take a good chunk of her remaining cash.

"Let me think about it," Emily told him. "I'm going to grab something quick for lunch. I'll stop by after and let you know what I decide."

"Cool." He smiled. "I'll set it aside…just in case."

She crunched the numbers in her head as she strode the short distance to Cuppa Joe. The popular coffee shop, located just off Main Street, was known for its excellent coffee selection and melt-in-your-mouth sourdough cinnamon rolls. It had recently added pizza by the slice to its limited lunch menu.

Stepping inside the shop, Emily reveled in the enveloping warmth and the wonderful smells. Yeast and cinnamon, rich roasted coffee and the enticing scent of sugar had her smiling as she approached the counter.

Though she knew the shop did a booming business, she'd missed the lunch rush. At this time of day, there was no line and plenty of open tables.

After receiving her order, Emily took her slice of pizza and complimentary cup of water to a small table by the fireplace, currently boasting faux fire logs instead of wood.

Emily studied the flickering flames and decided that fake or not, they added to the ambience without the need for actual firewood or generating heat.

When she pulled out the chair, her heart gave a little leap as she spotted the newspaper.

"Hey, let me wipe off the table before you sit." A teenage boy hurriedly stepped to the two-top. "I can recycle that paper for you."

"Actually, I'd like to keep it, if that's okay." Subscribing to the online newspaper was on Emily's list of things to do. Right after she obtained a credit card.

"Fine by me." The boy's lips quirked upward. "Gus, he's one of our regulars, always brings his paper from home with him. He reads it with his coffee, then leaves it for whoever wants it. I've tried to tell him that if someone does read the paper, they read it online, but he insists there are still people like him who prefer the real deal."

The boy chuckled, telling Emily exactly what he thought of that notion.

Tucking the newspaper under her arm, Emily lifted the plate and cup while the boy made a quick swipe of the table, which had appeared clean, but apparently wasn't.

"Thank you." She smiled at the boy as she took a seat.

"No prob."

Staring into the fake flickering flames, Emily sat back, took a big bite of pepperoni pizza, followed by a long drink of water.

At the nearby table, two older women were talking about the Antiques Extravaganza at the fairgrounds.

Emily set down her cup. She'd forgotten that was today. She and Beverly had planned to go together.

She could see it now, the two of them laughing and talking as they strolled up one aisle and down the other. Geraldine would have stayed home. Every year, she made it clear, in her nononsense way, that she didn't have any use for "old junk."

Lisa wasn't big on antiques, and Rosemary was too immersed in wedding plans to go this year.

It would have been fun, Emily thought wistfully. After checking out all the "old junk," she and Beverly would have enjoyed a leisurely lunch together.

They would eat and talk and laugh...

Emily's heart twisted. Could she go to the event alone? Or would it be a painful reminder of all she'd lost?

There was another possibility. She could use the free day pass she'd been given while at Vertical Ascent. It was to a fitness center that had recently opened. While checking out the exercise equipment would be fun, it was the pool—or rather, pools—that interested Emily.

She'd yet to put on the cute bikini she'd purchased on her trip to Gateway Promenade. She could swim laps, splash in the water or simply sit in a deck chair with a cool drink in one hand and a book in the other.

If only she had someone to go with...

As if Emily thinking of her had conjured her up, Chloe strode into the coffee shop.

She didn't appear to notice Emily as she headed straight to the counter to order.

Once Chloe had ordered, Emily sauntered over and tapped her on the shoulder.

Chloe jumped, and her gaze jerked up from the phone in her hand. "Oh, Emily, hello. Give me a sec."

After finishing her text, Chloe pocketed the phone. "I didn't notice you."

Emily gestured to the bag that now held the phone. "Something important? I mean, you seemed really engrossed."

"Not really. Jaclyn and I are trying to decide what we want to do this afternoon."

Room for one more? Emily wanted to ask, but didn't. While she had the feeling Chloe might not mind, Jaclyn was a different story.

"What did you come up with?" Emily tried for nonchalant.

"Nothing yet. I mean, we're going clubbing tonight, but we still haven't firmed up this afternoon." Chloe inclined her head. "What about you? Got big plans?"

"I went to the event at Culler Lake this morning." Emily gestured to the table by the fireplace. "After I eat my slice of pizza, I'm going to buy a bicycle."

"That sounds like fun."

"Chloe," the barista called out.

Chloe lifted her drink from the counter, then turned back to Emily. "Would you mind if I joined you for a few? Jaclyn is coming by to pick me up, but she had a couple things to finish up, so I'm not sure how long—"

"I'd love company." Emily hoped her smile didn't shine too brightly.

Once they sat, Chloe's gaze dropped to the *GraceTown Gazette* that Emily hadn't had a chance to read. A sadness filled her eyes. "Oh, Til."

For a second, Emily thought Chloe was speaking to her. Then she followed the direction of her gaze.

Emily blinked at the sight of the photograph of her with the headline Longtime Civic Leader Found Dead.

For several seconds, Emily simply stared at the article and the photo. She forced herself to breathe in and out.

"That was my friend who died." Chloe gestured with her hand toward the newspaper. "Matilda Beemis."

"I remember when Jaclyn gave you the news." Emily licked suddenly dry lips, her pulse fluttering like a hummingbird on steroids. "I hope it's okay to ask this, but how are you doing with all this? You mentioned she was like your grandmother…"

"She was." Sadness swept across Chloe's pretty face, and tears filled her eyes.

Emily folded up the newspaper, then stashed it in her bag to read later, keeping her gaze focused on Chloe.

Blinking back the tears, Chloe took a long sip of her drink. "I got the honey lavender latte. Next time you come here, you should try it. It's really good."

"I'll have to do that." Emily didn't want to talk about lavender lattes—which actually sounded gross to her—she wanted to let Chloe know it was okay to own and express her feelings. If she wanted to, that was.

"You know, my dad died not too long ago," Emily began, "and people always seemed to think that they couldn't talk about him, that making me remember him would cause me pain. What they never understood was that I was always remembering him, always thinking about him, whether or not they brought him up. In fact, I like sharing memories of him with others. It's a way of keeping him with me."

Chloe hesitated for only a second. "When I went away to college, Til and I didn't see each other much, but she wrote to me every week. Actual letters, not emails. My roommates couldn't believe I got real letters in the mail."

Emily said nothing, a sick ball forming in the pit of her stomach. She'd enjoyed writing to Chloe. Despite not receiving more than a handful of letters over those years in return, she'd kept writing.

"My roommates teased me, but I liked getting them," Chloe admitted. "Til was active and interested in so many things, not like a lot of older people."

Hearing the love and admiration in her voice had Emily taking a long drink of water, her throat suddenly parched.

Chloe's smile turned rueful. "I wasn't good about getting back to her. When I graduated and started my job in Miami, I was even worse. But whenever I visited GraceTown and we got together, it was as if I'd never left. Til never ragged on me about not staying in touch, not like my parents."

"You were busy."

"I was, and I, well, I got involved with a guy in Miami. I thought he was the one." Chloe gave a humorless chuckle. "Wasn't."

Emily straightened in her chair, a thousand questions crowding on the tip of her tongue. How was it that she hadn't known Chloe had been involved with someone in Miami? "Is that why you moved back here? Because that relationship ended?"

She hoped that wasn't too personal a question for a casual acquaintance to ask.

"Partially." After a moment of silence, Chloe admitted, "Mostly. When I returned to GraceTown, I wanted to hang with Til, but you know how it is—getting a place and starting a new job kept me busy. I thought we'd have time…" Chloe looked away, her expression suddenly bleak. "She probably died thinking I didn't care."

I know you cared.

The words nearly made it past her lips when Emily pulled them back. "I'm betting she knew."

Chloe's gaze returned to her. "Why do you think that?"

"Mostly because I believe that when we love someone, deep down, they sense it. The same way we know how they feel."

Chloe expelled a breath. "I hope that's true."

"No doubts."

"You remind me of her, you know."

"I do?"

"Not in looks, but in the way you talk, the way your words come together…" Chloe gave a little laugh. "Or maybe that's just me projecting."

"Sounds like your friend was a special lady."

"She was."

"You'll be attending her funeral." Emily said it as a statement, not a question.

Chloe sighed. "They aren't having one."

Emily bobbled the cup of water in her hand, but brought it quickly under control. With forced nonchalance, she took a long drink and reminded herself that that was what she had wanted. How many times had she told her friends that when she passed, she wanted no muss or fuss?

Now, seeing Chloe's grief, she wondered if she'd been wrong to deny those who'd been a part of her life the chance to say good-bye.

"Til didn't want one." Chloe absently shredded a napkin. "Though I've heard her friends are organizing a celebration of life to be held later this summer."

A warmth flowed through Emily's veins. "That sounds nice."

"There's also talk about renovating Maplewood Park in her memory."

"Isn't that the park where they found her body?"

"That's the one. She liked to go there and read. " Chloe chuckled and shook her head. "God knows why. The place is a dump. But she loved it just the same…"

Chloe's voice broke, and once again she blinked rapidly against tears that threatened to spill. "Sorry."

In that moment, Emily wanted nothing more than to take Chloe in her arms and hold her close, like she had when Chloe was young. Instead, she spoke in a low tone designed to soothe. "Give it time. Take all the time you need. There is no timetable on grief."

"You understand. Because of your dad, you understand." Chloe met Emily's gaze. "Jaclyn has never lost anyone. She can't understand why I'm still sad. She thinks I should be over it by now."

Going with emotion, Emily reached over and gave Chloe's hand a squeeze. "Grief doesn't work that way."

"No. No, it doesn't. I will miss Til forever." Chloe's voice thickened. Then, blinking rapidly, she took a long drink of her latte and appeared to steady. "She, ah, she left me her house."

Emily widened her eyes as if surprised. "That was nice of her."

"I didn't expect it." Chloe's gaze turned distant. "I thought everything would go to her charities."

"You were special to her." Emily spoke carefully. "Have you been to the house?"

"I've been tending to the garden, but I haven't gone inside." Chloe hesitated. "I don't want to go alone. Not the first time."

"Maybe you could take Jaclyn with you."

"I asked." Chloe shook her head. "She's not interested."

Not even for a friend? Emily nearly spoke the question aloud, but stopped herself just in time.

"If you, ah, if you'd like me to go with you sometime, I will."

"Thank you." Chloe's smile arrowed straight to Emily's heart. "I'll take you up—"

"There you are." Jaclyn's voice had them both jumping. Her gaze shifted from Emily to Chloe. "I thought you'd be waiting outside."

Chloe rose. "I craved a latte and ran into Emily. She kept me company while I waited."

"How nice." Jaclyn's smile didn't quite reach her eyes. "I'm parked in the loading zone."

"What fun activity do you two have planned for this afternoon?" Emily asked.

Jaclyn shrugged. "We haven't decided."

"There's the Antiques Extravaganza at the fairgrounds," Emily suggested.

Jaclyn laughed. "And mingle with a bunch of white-hairs? Ah, no, thank you."

"We'll figure something out," Chloe assured Jaclyn.

Jaclyn smiled back. "We always do."

"See you later, Emily," Chloe called over her shoulder as she hurried to catch up with her friend, who had turned and was nearly to the door.

Until Jaclyn's comment, Emily had been seriously considering the Antiques Extravaganza. Attending was something Til would have definitely done.

But she wasn't Til. She was Emily now. So why was she stuck in the past, rather than doing something different and fun?

Thinking of her bikini and the free pass to the fitness center had Emily finishing off the last bite of her pizza.

She would buy the bike, then head back to the hotel to change.

This was a new her, and it was time to take advantage of all that being young had to offer.

CHAPTER EIGHT

That night, Emily chose a flirty dress in an azure blue that flattered her peaches-and-cream complexion. She noticed her afternoon spent poolside—or maybe it was her time on the paddleboard—had given her a nice tan.

After contemplating several options, she added heeled sandals with a touch of bling, then stepped in front of the full-length mirror.

Staring at her reflection, she applied more color to her lips, then smiled in satisfaction. She was ready for dancing, drinking and a whole lot of fun.

Although Destiny was less than two miles away, it wouldn't be a pleasant trek in these shoes. She had the Uber driver let her off a block from the club, wanting to savor a few more minutes of the glorious weather before stepping inside.

It was funny that, until recently, she'd never realized just how much she loved being outdoors. Much of her life had been spent inside, first at the hotel working side by side with her father, then in various classrooms.

Was this love of the great outdoors something new? Emily mentally shook her head at the thought. Hadn't she been planning to sit in Maplewood Park and read when she'd run into Serena? And her large garden was a source of pride.

She thought of what Chloe had said about tending to her garden. A smile lifted her lips. Her flowers and vegetables were in good hands.

"Hey, pretty lady."

The voice came from a young man—okay, maybe not all that young compared to the new her, early twenties maybe—but that still seemed young to her. It was going to take a while, she realized, for her to accept her youth.

With a mass of dark hair on the top of his head and shaved sides, he stood watching her from beneath hooded eyes.

Emily studied him for a long moment and realized she knew him. Or rather, knew his grandmother. She pointed to him, finding pleasure in the knowledge. "I know you."

Apparently taking that as an invitation, he stepped closer. "Well, I'd like to know you a whole lot better."

"You're Donna Jacoby's grandson, Timmy." Emily smiled, thinking of the stories fellow teacher Donna had told about her grandson. *All boy* was how Donna had referred to his antics.

"It's TJ," he said stiffly.

"Your grandmother apparently hasn't gotten that message." Sympathy filled Emily's voice. Even after she'd gone by Til for years and made it clear that's what she wanted to be called, her grandmother in Michigan had always sent letters addressed to Matilda.

His gaze narrowed. "How do you know my granny?"

"Not important." Emily offered him a smile. "I'll be sure to tell her I ran into you."

"No need—" he began.

She strolled to the club entrance without looking back. Though she hadn't dated in sixty-plus years, Emily knew when a man was about to make a move on her.

As she wasn't the least bit interested in Timmy, especially

after hearing some of Donna's stories about him, she had needed to shut down any interest on his part. Introducing his grandmother into the conversation had seemed the easiest solution.

When Emily reached the outside of the club, she hesitated. What if no one spoke to her? Or asked her to dance?

She mentally shook off the worry. This uncertainty wasn't like her.

Pulling out her driver's license, Emily stepped to the man with the full beard and sleeve tats checking IDs. She recognized him from his job at the Crab Shack. "Good to see you, Dirk. I wasn't aware you also worked here."

Puzzlement filled his eyes as he studied her identification, then stamped her hand. "Have we met?"

"I'm in love with the food at the Crab Shack." For years, Emily and her friends had had a standing weekly dinner date at the seafood café. "I've seen you there."

After giving her a slow head-to-toe perusal, he shook his head slowly. "Naw, I'd remember you."

"Apparently not."

Dirk's gaze remained puzzled, and he repeated, "I'd remember you."

Emily only shot him a sunny smile before stepping through the open door.

Once inside, she checked out the club, winding her way through tables and the bar area with its endless stools, then past the stage, where a band tuned up. She didn't see Mackenna as she returned to the tables area, but stopped when a hand touched her arm.

She whirled to find Chloe grinning at her.

"I thought that was you." Chloe turned to Jaclyn. "Didn't I tell you I thought that was Emily?"

"You did," Jaclyn admitted. "Hi, Emily. Cute dress."

"Thanks."

"If you're not sitting with anyone, we have room at our table." Chloe pointed to an empty chair next to her.

Emily's heart gave an excited leap, but she kept her voice casual. "Thanks. The person I thought would be here apparently decided not to come."

"Happens." Chloe spoke matter-of-factly.

Before dropping down, Emily offered Jaclyn a hesitant smile. "If you don't mind."

"Not at all." Jaclyn waved a hand. "The more, the merrier."

Emily realized the two women were enjoying a night on the town with a large group of friends. A group that included men as well as women. At the far end of the table, Emily recognized Sophie and her husband, Joe, as well as Charlie and Hannah Rogan.

But no Mackenna, who was a friend of Hannah's. Finding her no longer seemed important, though if their paths did cross, Emily would definitely buy her that promised drink.

"Jaclyn was about to tell me about the date she had last night," Chloe said to Emily before turning her attention to her friend.

"We had fun, I guess." Jaclyn lifted a shoulder, then let it drop. "But no spark, know what I mean?"

Chloe nodded.

"I do, but I don't." Emily hadn't meant to speak. This wasn't her conversation, after all, but now both Chloe and Jaclyn were looking at her, and she felt she had to continue.

Emily strove for a casual tone instead of embarrassed. "I haven't had a lot of experience with guys," she confessed. "I've only kissed one man in my entire life."

Chloe laughed as if Emily had made a joke.

Jaclyn's blue eyes narrowed. "Are you playing us?"

"I'm not." Heat rose up her neck, but Emily was powerless to stop it.

"How can that be?" Chloe asked, her eyes wide.

"Juilliard is very competitive. I didn't have time for much

else." Sticking as close to the truth as possible, Emily continued. "I was engaged once. Vince was my first boyfriend and the only man I've ever kissed. When we broke up, I didn't feel much like dating."

"Or kissing." Jaclyn's lips quirked up.

"Are you ready now?" Excitement lit a fire in Chloe's amber eyes. "Do you have someone in mind who can help end the drought?"

"Not really." Emily resisted the urge to sigh.

"So the field is wide open?" Chloe clasped her hands together. "I love this."

"I'm glad one of us is excited." Emily rolled her eyes, though she had to admit she found Chloe's enthusiasm contagious.

"Let's make three kisses your goal for tonight. That's easily doable. Especially the closer it gets to closing." Chloe slung an arm around Emily's shoulders. "Trust me, by the time this evening is over, you won't be a kissing virgin."

"Kissing virgin?"

In response to the deep male voice, the three of them turned as one.

"Dalton." A startled look crossed Chloe's face, then she smiled. "Jaclyn didn't mention you were coming tonight."

"The sister is always the last to know." Jaclyn spoke in a droll tone before gesturing to Emily with an airy hand. "Emily Curtis, this eavesdropper is my brother, Dalton."

It was easy to see the family resemblance, as both siblings had dark-as-midnight hair and vivid blue eyes.

"It's nice to meet you, Emily." Dalton's gaze slid back to his sister. "My sister is a kissing virgin?"

Jaclyn laughed. "Not me. Emily."

"I've kissed a man before." Emily's cheeks burned. "Not that it's any of—"

"Whoa, hold up, Emily." Chloe's expression brightened. "Dalton may be able to help you out."

"Sure." His gaze shifted from one to the other. "Happy to help. What do I need to do?"

"Kiss Emily." Chloe spoke at the same instant Emily said, "Nothing."

"She's only kissed *one* guy." Disbelief rang in Chloe's voice. "Jaclyn and I will put an end to that tonight. We're going to find three men for her to kiss before closing."

"Three? Seriously?" Dalton asked.

"It's not that many." Chloe arched a brow. "What part are you finding difficult to understand, Dalton?"

"That someone this beautiful has only kissed one man." Dalton shook his head, then refocused on Emily. "What kind of guys have you been spending time with?"

"I haven't." Emily was not going to go into detail. She didn't owe him, or any other stranger, an explanation. "I've been busy with...life."

Dalton shifted his gaze to Chloe. "Unless she wants to kiss a bunch of different guys, it's not your business to intervene."

"She does want that." Jaclyn pinned Emily with her gaze. "Don't you?"

Emily wished, wished, wished that she had kept her mouth shut.

"I wouldn't mind getting a little practice." Emily could have cheered when her voice came out casual and offhand, just as she'd intended. "I just haven't seen anyone who strikes my fancy."

"Strikes your fancy?" Jaclyn gave a hoot of laughter. "That sounds like something my gran would say."

Thankfully, a response was unnecessary, because the band out of DC started up their set, and they were loud. It wasn't only the noise factor. Emily quickly discovered that this group was much more interested in dancing and drinking than talking.

So, Emily danced, flitting from one partner to another. She'd just returned to her seat after dancing with several guys when

Andrew Doman, a graduate student who worked part time at Timeless Treasures, approached her.

Whenever she'd stopped by the antique store as Til, she had always enjoyed her conversations with the serious young man, whose dark glasses had a habit of sliding down his nose.

After clearing his throat loudly, he asked her to dance.

As Emily could tell he was nervous, she offered him her brightest smile. "I'd love to."

A startled look crossed his face. Only then did she realize he'd been braced for rejection.

She took his arm and leaned close so he could hear her. "You work at Timeless Treasures."

"I do, but I've never seen you there. I would have remembered." His hazel eyes held an earnestness that tugged at her heart.

"I don't stop in often," she assured him, "and it wasn't any time recent."

That was it for talking now, since they'd reached the dance floor and were enveloped by the pounding beat. Emily found herself scattering smiles like confetti as she let the music take over.

Emily loved the way the music and the lyrics reached inside her body to wrap around her heart. She enjoyed moving to the beat, but found she missed being twirled around the floor in a man's arms.

She was nearly back to her seat when the band began a slow set. Emily's heart gave a little leap. Perhaps she and Chloe would now have a chance to say more than one or two words to each other.

A brown-haired young man with a full goatee reached the table right before Emily. He held out a hand to Chloe. "They're playing our song, babe."

Rising, Chloe took his hand, then wrapped her arms around his neck and kissed him passionately.

Emily's eyes widened at the bold gesture even as she fought a pang of envy.

Jaclyn soon joined her friend on the floor with a tall guy who had a messy mop of blond hair. Emily had noticed the two sharing other dances together.

"Care to dance?"

Emily looked up, and there was Josh from the Dairy Sweet. "I suppose if I can't have a peach ice cream cone, I'll settle for a dance."

"Always second choice." Josh gave an exaggerated sigh as they made their way through the crowd.

When they reached the dance floor and he held out his hand, she took it and placed her left hand on top of his right shoulder.

Josh was an excellent dancer. Instead of simply swaying to the music, like Jaclyn and Chloe were doing with their partners, his feet and hers moved in well-synchronized movements.

It had been so long since she'd danced in this manner that having her hand clasped in his felt oddly intimate. Emily soon lost herself in the music, in the sensation of his skin against hers, in the intoxicating scent of a citrusy cologne and a warm body only inches from hers.

"Kiss him," Jaclyn hissed.

Emily turned her head to see Jaclyn and her date dance off.

"What did she say?" Josh asked, though his eyes shining with amusement told her he'd understood the directive.

"My friends have this game where they've challenged me to kiss three guys before the end of the evening."

"How's that going?"

"Big fat zero," she told him.

"I'm happy to get you closer to the end zone."

"You'd do that for me?"

"And for myself." He tucked a stray strand of hair behind her ear. "Interested?"

"Sure." She smiled. "I—"

She didn't have time to finish what she was about to say when his lips closed over hers in a soft, sweet kiss.

"Thank you," she told him when he pulled back.

"Is it three kisses with three different guys or three kisses from the same guy?" His eyes twinkled. "Because if it's three by the same guy, I'm your man."

The song ended, and it would have been so easy to stay in those arms and dance to another song, but she didn't want to give Josh the wrong impression. She liked Josh, enjoyed talking to him, but like Jaclyn's date last night, there was no spark.

"Thanks for the dance." She stepped back. "And the kiss."

"I'm totally serious when I say it was my pleasure."

Emily crossed the goal line by garnering two more kisses before the end of the evening—one with a young guy who'd just graduated from Collister College and was planning on moving to New York, the other with a man who looked a decade older than most of the guys in the club.

Earlier in the evening, she'd considered kissing Andrew, but worried he might read something into it, so the guy with the mustache had gotten the nod instead.

The last thing she wanted to do was to lead anyone on. She caught Jaclyn's brother watching her, but he didn't approach.

Probably afraid I'll jump him, Emily thought with a smile.

"Last call," Jaclyn announced, her gaze shifting from Emily to Chloe. "Either of you want anything?"

"I'm fine." Emily stood. "I need to call an Uber."

"Don't do that." Chloe rose and put a restraining hand on Emily's arm before turning to Jaclyn. "We can give her a ride home, right?"

The question in Chloe's voice told Emily that Jaclyn was the one who'd driven tonight.

"Sure." Jaclyn stood and smiled. "Anyone who crosses the goal line deserves better than an Uber."

CHAPTER NINE

Tuesday afternoon, Emily received a text from Chloe asking if she was available to go with her to Til's house.

Excitement surged, and her fingers trembled as she quickly texted her reply.

Chloe arrived at four, pulling to the curb in front of the hotel and slanting Emily a sideways glance as she slid into the passenger seat. "I hope this works for you."

Though Chloe's smile was bright, Emily saw lines of tension around her eyes. "It works perfectly."

"I heard you've been playing in the town square around this time."

Obviously, Chloe wanted to keep the discussion off the house. Which was okay with Emily. "I've tried different times and days, but I've discovered that over the lunch hour works best. I've been thinking of setting a specific time and day of the week so those who like to listen will know I'll be there."

Chloe's fingers, holding the steering wheel in a death grip, relaxed. "That's smart."

Emily's lips twisted into a wry smile. "Of course, a job will put an end to busking, at least during the day."

The stop at a traffic light had Chloe shifting to face Emily. "Job? You got a job? Where?"

"Not yet. But I put in an application with the school system. While I don't have a teaching certificate, I do have a BFA and lots of music experience."

"I bet they'll hire you." Chloe offered a supportive smile. "You'll make a wonderful teacher. They'd be lucky to have you."

"Thank you for that."

The light changing to green had Chloe shifting her eyes straight ahead. "But school doesn't start until August. Can you make it that long without a job?"

"If I have to. Besides, August isn't that far off. I mean, it's nearly July. And teachers usually start a couple weeks before the students."

"You seem to know a lot about teaching already."

"I did my research."

"What if you don't get the job?" Chloe then rushed to add, "Though I'm sure you will."

"I don't know." The not knowing had caused Emily a moment of panic. "Private lessons, both in person and online, are a possibility. I'm sure there are other options I haven't thought of yet."

The truth was, Emily had been having too much fun for the past week to consider what she was going to do with the rest of her life. But as the money she'd rescued from the coffee can grew smaller, the need to find something—anything—grew more urgent.

"I also need to find somewhere other than the hotel to live." Emily kept her tone casual, knowing that Chloe and Jaclyn had a roommate who'd recently moved out. "You don't know of anyone looking for a roommate, do you?"

Chloe appeared to consider, then shook her head. "Tia—she was our roommate—recently moved in with her boyfriend, but Jaclyn doesn't want to replace her. In fact, I think she'll go solo when I move into Til's house."

"You're moving into Til's house?" Why had Emily not considered that? Why had she thought Chloe would sell the home and buy something more modern?

"I'm thinking about it." The lines of tension had returned to bracket Chloe's mouth and eyes.

It didn't surprise Emily that Arthur Louden, the attorney handling the estate, had given Chloe the key. Til had put the house in a trust to go to Chloe upon her death, bypassing the need for probate.

Chloe pulled into the driveway and cut the engine. Neither of them made a move to get out of the vehicle.

Emily studied the bungalow that had been her home for decades. "That's a nice house."

A soft look filled Chloe's amber eyes. "Til took such good care of it. I mean, it's not a mansion or anything, but, like you said, it's nice."

As Chloe seemed in no hurry to get out, Emily relaxed back against the leather seat. It struck her that, like Chloe, she needed a few minutes to settle before entering the home.

"I want to do the walk-through." Chloe expelled a breath. "The thing is, I know doing that will stir up all sorts of memories."

"Good and bad?" Emily kept her voice light.

Chloe gave a little laugh and shook her head. "Only good. There are no bad memories in this house. Unless you count that Til is no longer here."

The sadness on Chloe's face tugged at Emily's heartstrings. "You're missing her today."

Chloe pushed open the car door. "I miss her every day."

Emily shot a quick glance at the single-stall garage and thought longingly of the five-year-old sedan sitting inside with only 30,000 miles. Unfortunately, it was now out of her reach.

Instead of going inside, when Chloe reached the porch, she dropped to sit on the glider.

Following her lead, Emily sat on the other end of the turquoise and white glider that had graced her front porch for the last thirty years.

Once seated, she shifted her body in Chloe's direction. "I love these."

For a second, Chloe looked confused, then she smiled. "Oh, the glider. Yeah, it's great."

Chloe gave a little push with her foot, and thanks to the WD-40 that Emily had used only days before she'd met Serena in the park, the glider slid silently back and forth.

"Before I texted you, I asked Jaclyn again if she wanted to come with me this afternoon." Chloe spoke almost to herself, her attention now focused on a hanging basket of red geraniums that appeared to have been watered recently. "I had the afternoon off, and so did she."

Emily said nothing.

Chloe's gaze abruptly shifted back, her eyes meeting Emily's. "I know Jaclyn can come across as unlikable, but she's protective of her friends and a really good person deep down."

When Emily gave only a noncommittal smile, Chloe continued.

"I think the real reason she didn't want to come with me is because she knew I'd get emotional." Tears filled Chloe's eyes. "Looks like she was right."

Emily laid a hand on Chloe's shoulder. "You can cry all you want around me. When my father had his first stroke, anytime anyone asked how he was doing, I'd dissolve in a puddle of tears."

"You don't seem like the puddle-of-tears type." Chloe's lips quirked upward.

"I loved him," Emily said simply. "Seeing him hurt, hurt me."

Chloe nodded, and Emily saw understanding in the amber depths. Then her gaze shifted to the front door. She stood. "It's time."

It's strange to walk through your own house, Emily thought, trying to see it through the eyes of a stranger. She was glad she had tidied up before leaving for the card party that final day.

The print she'd purchased so long ago at ARTistry in the Park, an archival-quality print of Andrew Wyeth's *Christina's World*, hung on the wall.

Emily had been drawn to the image that many saw as depicting the strength of Andrew's neighbor in Maine who was unable to walk.

Chloe didn't even glance at the print as she walked through the living room, her hand brushing the multicolored crocheted throw lying across the back of the sofa.

Emily wondered, but didn't ask, if Chloe remembered that time when they'd sat on the sofa and crocheted the little squares when she was eleven. How proud they'd both been when they'd put the squares together.

She'd wanted Chloe to take the afghan home with her. Chloe had refused, saying it didn't fit her mother's décor and would likely end up getting tossed out.

Chloe moved to the sideboard, her lips lifting in a soft smile as she studied the framed photograph of her and Til holding up the certificates that they'd received for their volunteer efforts one long-ago summer.

Though Chloe, at fourteen, hadn't really been old enough to volunteer, that was the year she'd spent the entire summer with Til. There were only so many leisure activities one could do.

As volunteerism was a big part of Til's life, she'd wanted to share that experience with Chloe. And, in the process, hopefully instill that same love in the young girl.

"What are those certificates you're holding?" Emily asked by way of bringing up the topic.

"Volunteer Appreciation." Chloe's smile had the sadness leaving her eyes. "Til would work with the families of newly arrived seasonal workers on building their language skills. While she was with the mom or dad, I would be on the other side of the room having a conversation in English with the children."

"How did you like it?"

"I had a blast. Often, at the beginning, I could tell the kids worried I was going to be mean and critical, but they quickly discovered I was there to applaud their efforts and bolster their confidence."

Emily hid a smile, recognizing the words she'd said to the younger Chloe.

"Do you do any volunteering now?" Emily tossed out the comment much as a fisherman would toss a hook into the water. Then she waited.

"I haven't. When I was in school, well, I was too busy. In Miami, it never happened." A thoughtful look crossed Chloe's face. "I could make it work now."

"There's always a need." At Chloe's quick glance, she added, "I've done it in the past. Though I can't make it work now, for obvious reasons, I found that giving back feels good. Does that sound weird?"

The first natural smile she'd seen on Chloe's lips since they'd entered the house blossomed. "Not weird at all. In fact, it sounds like something Til would say."

Emily followed Chloe into the kitchen, a cheery room with wallpaper sporting a bright yellow floral print with green and yellow flowers.

"Wow." Emily forced a surprised tone. "Get a load of the wallpaper."

"I know." Chloe's eyes softened with remembrance. "Definitely retro."

"I bet that'll be one of the first things you change." Emily loved the brightness of the paper. On gloomy days when the outside skies had been gray, simply walking into the kitchen in the morning had brightened her mood.

Chloe turned, her eyes widening in surprise. "I'm not changing it."

"You're not?"

"I love this house just the way it is." Chloe's gaze settled on the black wall clock in the shape of a cat. She pointed. "When I was little, I loved to eat my cereal and watch his eyes and tail move back and forth."

Emily's only response was a smile. She'd loved watching the cat every morning, too.

"Each room in this house holds many wonderful memories." Chloe's gaze shifted to her. "Why would I want to make changes?"

"I just thought you'd want to, I don't know, maybe put your own mark on the house?" While the knowledge that Chloe wasn't planning to gut her home pleased her, Emily also wanted Chloe to enjoy her new home.

"Maybe, in time, but I'm in no hurry."

"This house has, what, two bedrooms?"

"Yes. Til used the spare as a sewing room when I wasn't spending the night." Chloe paused, then shook her head. "I don't need to see those. They haven't changed since I was a kid."

Pushing the back door open, Chloe stepped into the attached lean-to, scooping up a pair of gardening gloves on top of the shelves.

"Do you have another pair?"

Chloe whirled. "What did you say?"

"I-I was just wondering if there's another pair of gloves." Emily shifted uncertainly from one foot to the other, not understanding the look on Chloe's face. "If you're going to do some gardening, I'd like to help."

Expelling a ragged breath, Chloe bent over. Pulling open a drawer in the cabinet where Til kept extra supplies, she grabbed a pair of gloves and tossed them to her.

"Did I say something wrong?" Emily asked, wondering at the

odd response.

"No." Lifting her hands, Chloe shook them back and forth. "It's just, that was my line."

"Your line?"

"Til would grab her gloves, and I would always say, 'Do you have another pair?'" Chloe gave an embarrassed laugh. "I know it's silly, but in that moment, I could see the two of us and—" Biting her lip and blinking rapidly, Chloe turned away and stepped into the yard.

Emily followed her out the back door. The second her gaze swept the yard, Emily felt her heart rise to her throat. Instead of the shriveled plants and weed-filled mess she'd expected after so many days since her death, she saw a thriving vegetable garden and flowers—including her precious hollyhocks—in full bloom.

"I've kept things nice. I didn't want all of Til's work to be in vain." Pride filled Chloe's voice. "I thought I'd do just a little weeding today. It won't take long."

"I'm happy to help."

Chloe studied Emily, taking in the shorts and cotton T-shirt she wore as if seeing them for the first time. "Gardening can be a dirty job."

Emily flashed a smile. "Since when did a little dirt hurt anyone?"

They picked produce, then went to work weeding. Even though Chloe's efforts were clearly visible, at this time of year, weeds fought back.

As it had for decades, working in the dirt settled and soothed Emily. She and Chloe worked side by side in companionable silence.

"Til was my inspiration, you know."

Chloe's unexpected comment had Emily's hand freezing on the spade. "For?"

"So many things."

The minute of silence that followed had Emily remembering

all those times when Chloe had shared what was troubling her.

The conversations most often had occurred when she had been at the sink washing dishes while Chloe dried or when they had been working together in the garden, like they were now.

"When I was in Miami, I dated this guy, Paul."

Emily waited through fifteen long seconds of silence before tossing out, "You thought he might be *the one?*"

Chloe nodded and made a sound somewhere between a laugh and a scoff. "I did think that—early on, anyway."

"What did Til think of him?"

"I never mentioned him to her."

"Oh." Emily forced a little laugh. "I guess that was a silly question. Like you'd tell her about your love life."

Chloe's teeth sank into her lower lip. "I always did before, but Paul was my boss and fifteen years older than me. I knew she'd have concerns."

Emily only nodded.

"The thing is, without her even knowing about him, she was the one who helped me break it off." Chloe's eyes took on a distant look. "He could be charming, but he didn't treat me how I wanted to be treated. I realized I didn't have to settle for that. That's where Til came in."

"I'm confused. You said she didn't know about him."

"Til didn't need a man to be happy, for her life to be complete. She was open to romantic love, but it didn't happen, and she was okay with that. She had friends—good friends—and she enjoyed the life she built here in GraceTown. I realized that I, too, could be okay without a man."

Emily nodded. "Did you move back to GraceTown to get away from him?"

"Not at all. Paul and I were over long before I decided to move back. I returned because eventually I'd like to open a B&B here." Chloe stood and brushed the dirt off her jeans. "And mostly because no other place but here has ever felt like home."

CHAPTER TEN

By the time she and Chloe finished with the garden, they were both hungry. That's when Emily learned that Chloe had made plans to meet Jaclyn at the Crab Shack for a night of trivia and dinner.

"I know it sounds kind of lame," Chloe said when broaching the subject. "But the trivia is fun, and the food is awesome. Would you want to come with?"

Emily paused, not wanting to appear too eager. "Sure. That works for me."

"Let me text Jaclyn that we're on our way." Chloe pulled out her phone. "Hopefully, she can get us a table. They fill up quickly on Tuesday nights."

The popular seafood spot was indeed packed when she and Chloe arrived. What surprised Emily the most was the wide assortment of ages present for trivia night.

Though she and her friends had come here regularly, they'd always avoided Tuesday nights because of the crowds.

"Jaclyn brought the guy from the club." Emily's gaze slid from the blond man to the one with the goatee. "And the one you were dancing with."

"Garrett and Bradley," Chloe said, supplying the names. "Looks like Dalton is here, too. He must have invited himself."

Emily was glad Dalton was here, if only so she wouldn't feel so much like a third wheel.

While the other guys had dressed casually, Dalton looked like he'd jumped out of a *Fortune* 500 board meeting.

"What's with the suit and tie?" Chloe asked in lieu of a greeting when they reached the table and took a seat.

"All the department heads met with the provost today." Dalton loosened his tie. "The meeting went late."

"Provost?" Emily asked.

"Dalton is head of the Economics Department at Collister," Jaclyn answered before he could. "Think big fish, small pond."

"Thanks, dear sister." If Dalton was disturbed by her comment, it didn't show.

"Anytime." Jaclyn smiled at Emily. "My job as a sister is to keep him humble."

They moved on to introductions, and Emily learned Garrett worked for a local outfitter, and Bradley was in pharmaceutical sales.

They ordered, and their food arrived quickly, giving them thirty minutes to eat before the trivia began. As Jaclyn and Chloe were giving the guys their full attention, that left Emily with Dalton.

"How's life at the Oasis Hotel?" Dalton picked up a fry and took a bite.

"I'm ready to find something more permanent." Emily forked off a bite of her catfish, fried just the way she liked it, the flavor of Old Bay seasoning adding to the taste of the crispy batter. "You don't happen to know of any places for rent? I'd really like something I could move into right away."

Dalton rubbed his chin, his eyes turning thoughtful. "No, and I think it will be difficult finding something available before the first of the month."

"I have no doubt that's true, but I'm holding on to hope something will turn up."

"What are you looking for?"

"Studio or one-bedroom." Emily gave a little laugh. "Heck, at this point, I'd settle for a room and a shared bathroom."

"You are desperate."

"Not desperate." Emily kept her tone light. "But I can't afford to stay much longer at the Oasis. I need something cheaper."

"What is it you do for work?" Dalton asked. "I don't believe anyone has said."

"I was the concertmaster with the Baltimore Symphony Orchestra." Emily sipped her Coke. "Right now, I'm unemployed. But I'm looking, and I'm sure something will turn up."

"I applaud your confidence."

Even as she basked in the warmth of his smile, they both knew that a positive attitude didn't always ensure success. Achieving success took hard work and determination. Other than applying with the school system, she hadn't been doing the work.

That ends today, she told herself. Tomorrow she would make a list of possibilities and start working that list.

"Ladies and gentlemen," Dirk announced, "thank you for joining us tonight. It's that time again, time to add a bit of fun and challenge your brains with Tuesday Night Trivia." He waited for the applause to wind down before he continued.

"It's now time to pull out your phones and follow the directions on your screens." Dirk pointed to the large display on one wall. "Then get ready to put your thinking caps on. We have a number of tough, but exciting, questions for you to answer this evening. For those new to the party, each week the focus is different. For tonight, the questions will center around twentieth-century events. We've come up with ones that will not only test your knowledge, but hopefully keep you entertained. And the winner will have their meal and drink tab comped."

More cheers.

Across the table from her, Garrett groaned. "I sucked at history."

Emily experienced a rush of excitement. Twentieth-century events. Right up her alley.

"Before we dive in, I want to make sure everyone is ready. Are you up to the challenge?"

Hoots of "yes" and "let's get this party started!" filled the room.

Dirk grinned. "That's just what I want to hear. Let the trivia begin."

Thirty minutes later, Emily sat back in her chair and smiled in satisfaction.

"You really know your twentieth-century history." Admiration shone in Dalton's blue eyes.

Emily waved a hand, admiring again the candy pink of her nails. "It's a specialty of mine."

She'd won the trivia contest by a wide margin. The win had resulted in her fish meal and drink being free.

"Are you a history teacher?" Garrett asked, taking a sip of his beer.

"I'm a musician. I'll be busking in the town square during the lunch hour tomorrow. Right by the angel statue. You and Jaclyn should stop by."

Garrett exchanged a look with Jaclyn. "We have jobs."

"Your loss. I'm amazing, if I do say so myself." She shot him a cocky smile as she finished off her soda.

"Busking is your job? Your only job?" The look Bradley shot her was incredulous.

Emily wanted to say, *Just like pushing pills is your job*, but she refrained, knowing he had a point. It would be difficult to live off the money tossed into her violin case.

"Lay off her, Brad," Chloe told him.

"You can support yourself doing that?" Like a dog with a bone, Bradley couldn't seem to let it go.

The bartender showing up tableside with their bills saved Emily from having to respond.

At the sight of Dirk, Emily pretended to pout. "Don't tell me. You decided to charge me, after all."

Rocking back on his boot heels, Dirk shook his head. "I guess you really have come here before."

Dirk's comment had Dalton frowning in puzzlement.

"What do you mean by that?" Dalton asked.

"I ran into this guy last Saturday at Destiny." Emily offered Dirk a smile. "When I mentioned I've been here before, he didn't believe me."

Dirk held up a large, scarred hand. "I cannot believe I didn't remember you. How is that even possible?"

"I admit it's crazy," Emily teased, feeling lighthearted and flushed with triumph after her trivia victory, "since we both know I'm pretty unforgettable."

The bartender's lips quirked upward, and he chuckled. "Definitely. My bad."

"So is my tab still comped?" she asked.

"Did you win fair and square?"

"Absolutely." Other than, of course, having personal knowledge of the twentieth century because she'd lived through much of it.

"Then no charge for you, Blondie."

Emily studied Dirk for a long moment. "Do I get a congratulatory kiss, too?"

With that one question, Emily had recaptured the attention of everyone at the table.

"You go, girl," Jaclyn said.

Amusement skittered across Dirk's face. "If you want one, it's also on the house."

"In that case..." Pushing back her chair, Emily stood and

placed her lips firmly on Dirk's mouth. Because of his facial hair, it was a lot like kissing Vince. Then she stepped back. "Very nice."

Dirk's lips lifted in a slow smile. "If you want a repeat—"

"I'm good." She flashed a brilliant smile. "Thanks."

"No, thank *you*." Dirk chuckled and, after making sure no additional drinks were needed, laid down the individual checks and strolled off.

"How was it?" Jaclyn asked, her eyes as merry as Emily had ever seen them.

"Nice enough." Though her lips couldn't keep from curving, Emily shrugged.

"Why did you kiss him?" Garrett's expression was clearly puzzled.

"Umm, because I felt like it."

"We challenged Emily to kiss three different guys at Destiny on Saturday," Jaclyn explained. "It appears she decided to continue the challenge tonight."

Then, after looking around the table and realizing there were three men there whom Emily hadn't kissed, one who was with her, Jaclyn continued. "But just one guy tonight, right, Emily?"

"That's right," Emily concurred, seeing the warning in Jaclyn's eyes. "Just one tonight."

On Friday, when Chloe asked if she'd like to go to the county fair with her and Jaclyn that night, the offer came at exactly the right time.

Less than an hour earlier, Emily had received a letter from GraceTown Public Schools that she hadn't gotten the job. To her way of thinking, the fact that it was obviously a form letter only added insult to injury.

Emily had the feeling if Chloe hadn't texted, she might have spent the evening feeling sorry for herself. Which would have been a waste of a perfectly awesome summer day.

Tonight, she would cast aside any worries and simply have fun.

Though the fair was always a little dusty—when it wasn't muddy—and most attendees went ultra casual, Emily decided to go festive. She chose a short halter dress in mossy green and twisted her hair back into a kind of messy knot.

When Jaclyn's SUV pulled up in front of the Oasis, Emily practically skipped to the vehicle. She stopped abruptly when she spotted Mackenna sitting in the back seat.

"Hey, I know you." Mackenna pointed. "Jaclyn said we were picking up someone named Emily, but I didn't realize it was you."

Jaclyn's gaze shifted from Mackenna to her. "You know each other?"

"Mackenna was nice enough to give me a private paddleboard lesson last weekend," Emily explained.

"She didn't need much instructing," Mackenna told Jaclyn. "She's a natural."

The conversation on the drive to the fairgrounds had Emily learning that Mackenna's last name was Lee, she worked at Collister College in Marketing and Student Recruitment, and she had been friends with Jaclyn since high school.

Emily got the impression that while Makenna and Jaclyn were friends, they weren't tight, not like Jaclyn and Chloe.

Once they reached the fairgrounds, Emily and her three companions headed for the Midway. Though Emily wouldn't have minded meandering through the ag exhibits or swinging by the animal pens, filled with 4-H prize-winning stock, it was clear the others weren't interested.

She'd seen that the second she'd asked if there was anything in the ag buildings or exhibits that anyone wanted to check out.

"Are you kidding me?" Jaclyn had made a face. "I have two words for you. Dirty. Smelly."

Mackenna hadn't bothered to respond, but she was wearing a white dress that looked as if the dirt from the barns would leap on it like fleas off a mangy dog.

"Do *you* want to see the animals, Emily?" Chloe asked when they were nearly past the barns.

"Not really." Emily waved a dismissive hand. "I just didn't want to walk on by if anyone was interested."

"We only like the Midway." Jaclyn tossed the words over her shoulder. "That's where everyone will be tonight."

"Everyone who we want to see, anyway," Chloe quipped, and the other two laughed.

"Who are you hoping to see?" Emily asked, but Chloe had already turned back and was responding to something Jaclyn had said.

As they strolled by booths selling everything from turkey legs to fried pickles, the distance between her and the three began to feel as wide as the Grand Canyon. She felt like an afterthought as they spoke about people Emily didn't know and laughed over shared memories.

Emily listened, hoping to gain a better grasp of their interests, but the noise of the fair made hearing their conversation difficult. She thought she heard Chloe mention something about unique foods.

"I tried chocolate-covered bacon one time." Emily had tasted the unique food item just last year at Geraldine's urging.

She must have been close enough for the three to hear her, because as one they turned back.

"You ate what?" Jaclyn asked, her voice rising.

"Chocolate-covered bacon." Emily smiled, recalling that the nearly perfect sweet and salty blend had left her wanting more. "It's really good."

"Sounds yummy," Chloe admitted.

Jaclyn wrinkled her nose. "Oh please, Chloe. You and I both know it sounds gross."

Before Mackenna could weigh in with her opinion, Jaclyn brought up a party she'd attended in Baltimore last year where bacon had been an ingredient in cheese gougères.

An appetizer that only Emily had never tasted. Just like that, Emily found herself once again relegated to the nosebleed section.

Emily told herself to be patient. Building connections took time. The process couldn't be rushed. The trouble was, she wanted friends and that feeling of connection now.

The entrance to the Midway was in sight when they bumped into Garrett, Bradley and a guy Mackenna introduced as Wes.

While Wes was new to Emily, it appeared by the way he slung an arm around Mackenna's shoulders that the two knew each other very well.

Emily wondered if the three women had been hoping to meet up with these guys this evening.

"We came to check out the Midway," Jaclyn explained.

"Can we join you?" Garrett asked.

Jaclyn's arms wrapped around his neck, and she kissed him, giving him his answer without saying a word.

For Emily, nothing changed with the addition of the three guys—except, instead of trailing after three women, she now trailed after three couples.

Then, quite unexpectedly, Dalton appeared and fell into step beside her.

"What are you doing here?" she asked, unable to keep from smiling.

"Same as you, enjoying the fair." He gazed at the three couples who were so busy laughing and talking they hadn't once glanced back at her. Or him. "Or are you?"

Emily fought to remain positive. "The night is still young."

"Why did you come with three couples? Seems like tagging along wouldn't be much fun."

"I didn't tag along." Heat flooded her cheeks. "I came with

Jaclyn, Chloe and Mackenna. We ran into the guys a few minutes ago. I don't think it was planned, but I don't know for sure."

They'd reached the edge of the Midway when Chloe turned back, as if suddenly remembering Emily.

Her eyes widened at the sight of Dalton. "Hey, where did you come from?"

Dalton waved a hand. "I spotted Emily and came over to say hello. The rest of you were too busy talking to notice."

Everyone had turned by this time.

Jaclyn gave a little laugh. "I almost forgot Emily was with us."

"That was pretty obvious." Dalton shot his sister a pointed look.

"Emily doesn't need a keeper," Jaclyn began. "She—"

"Your sister is right. I don't need a keeper. In fact, I was thinking of doing a little exploring on my own." When Chloe opened her mouth as if to protest, Emily lifted a hand. "I want to see what's out there."

Chloe's expression brightened. "You're going on a manhunt."

For only a second, Emily was as confused as everyone else. Then she laughed. "Something like that."

It wasn't, of course, anything like that, but playing along saved face.

Jaclyn turned toward Makenna and the guys and quickly explained, "She's on a hunt for more men to kiss."

"Being with a group would be a definite deterrent," Mackenna agreed.

"Almost as bad as being here with your mom." Chloe made a face.

"Or your grandmother." Jaclyn laughed.

Garrett's arm dropped from Jaclyn's waist, his gaze now on Emily. "If you're looking for a guy to kiss, you can start with me."

The back of Jaclyn's hand slapping his midsection had him emitting a loud, "Oof."

"I was just kidding," Garrett protested.

"It didn't sound that way to me." Jaclyn's eyes flashed a warning. To him? To Emily?

Emily didn't want to wait around to find out.

"You guys have fun. I'll grab an Uber home. We'll catch up this weekend." Emily didn't wait for anyone to urge her to stay, which was good because even as she strolled off, she didn't hear any protests.

She'd gone a good ten feet before Dalton caught up to her.

"If you want to be alone, I'll leave, but if you'd like company, I'm available."

Emily hesitated, not wanting his pity.

"Unless you really are on a hunt for guys to kiss and are worried that I'll be in the way."

She looked at him, searching for what she wasn't sure. "You don't approve."

"It's not my decision. I support you doing whatever you want—your body, your life. I've just never been big on kissing strangers." Dalton offered a sheepish smile. "I'm a romantic. Old-fashioned, you might say. I like to take my time so that when I kiss someone, it means something. I don't want to be the guy a girl can kiss and forget. I want to be the guy she always thinks about."

"I've had enough with the kissing stuff." Emily waved an airy hand. "Kissing strangers can be fun, but like you said, it's not all that satisfying."

They walked in silence for several more feet.

"I was supposed to meet a group from my department tonight at the beer garden," Dalton said, breaking the silence.

"Well, don't let me keep you—"

"You're not." He spoke quickly. "I already swung by and glanced in before I spotted you. Wall-to-wall people. Not what I was looking for this evening."

"And the Midway is?"

He laughed. "That kid who loved all the sights and sounds

must still be in there, because I found myself drawn in this direction. I told myself that I'd walk around, maybe grab some chocolate-covered bacon and—"

"You overheard."

"Overheard what?" The puzzlement in his eyes was too real to be faked.

"You actually like chocolate-covered bacon?"

"Who wouldn't? I get it every year." He chuckled. "I know it sounds gross, but—"

"It's really yummy." Emily couldn't keep from smiling as she glanced around and breathed in the atmosphere.

"What's on your agenda for the evening?" he asked.

"I'm looking to simply enjoy the fair." She inclined her head. "What about you?"

"What sounds good to me is…" His head tipped back as his gaze lifted skyward. "A ride on a Ferris wheel with a pretty woman."

Then his vivid blue eyes were back on her. "Interested?"

CHAPTER ELEVEN

The lights from the giant wheel illuminated the night sky. Emily fought a shiver of excitement as she waited beside Dalton. Thankfully, the line moved swiftly, and it wasn't long until Emily sat beside him in a red cart.

The attendant, an older man with bad teeth, clicked the bar into place, then motioned to his coworker. The cart immediately gave a lurch and started its journey upward.

"I haven't been on one of these in ages." Emily sat back and breathed a happy sigh. "My friend Irene loved Ferris wheels. Whenever the fair came to town, it was the one ride we had to go on."

"Irene." Dalton rolled the name around on his tongue. "It's a beautiful name, but one you don't hear often."

"Haven't you heard?" Emily kept her tone light. "Old-fashioned names have been experiencing a resurgence."

He only smiled.

As the wheel jolted upward as each cart was filled, Emily leaned forward. She breathed in the sweet, fried goodness of funnel cakes, the enticing fragrance of barbecue smoke from the grills and the buttery and salty scent of popcorn.

The wonderful and diverse range of scents that contributed to the vibrant atmosphere had a wave of nostalgia washing over her.

From where she sat, looking out over GraceTown, it was as if nothing had changed. Yet everything had. At least in her world. "This is amazing."

When Dalton didn't reply, she turned in her seat and found him studying her. When her eyes met his, he smiled.

"You say that as if you're seeing it all for the first time."

"It feels that way." She returned his smile, then shifted her attention back to the sky. "I haven't always, you know, taken time to smell the roses."

Good humor lit his blue eyes. "I haven't heard that expression in a while."

"I was so focused on getting done what needed to be done and focusing on what others wanted that I neglected my own needs and wants and failed to fully appreciate everything around me."

Not saying a word, Dalton placed a hand over the top of the one she'd rested lightly on the bar.

For a second, Emily reveled in the warmth of his skin and the gentle support.

"I'm doing things differently now." Emily thought of all the activities she'd crammed into her life since that day in the park. "I'm making more time for fun, for me. And even more important, I'm savoring all the sweet, simple moments, like this one."

Emily spotted a family group down below. The littlest girl wore a crown and held a balloon sporting the image of a birthday cake.

The memories flooding back forced Emily to blink back sudden tears.

"What's wrong?" Dalton asked.

"Nothing. I was just thinking of my father and all the ways he showed me he cared. He wasn't one for parties, but each year on my birthday, he made sure we celebrated." She took a breath and let it out slowly. "I took so much for granted."

Dalton gave her hand a squeeze. "I think we're all guilty of that."

"I'm doing better at embracing moments now," Emily told him.

"My grandfather died last year." Dalton's eyes took on a distant look. "He was a great guy, the rock of our family. Though he wasn't the most demonstrative man, he showed his love to all of us in so many ways. Ways I took for granted."

"I read somewhere that we should consider mistakes stepping stones to wisdom."

"It's a good thought." Dalton nodded. "And, thankfully, we both have lots of time to learn those life lessons."

Emily nodded. The youth elixir had given her that time.

Dalton's arm slipped to rest lightly around her shoulders. As the wheel made a second and third rotation, she wondered what it would be like to kiss him.

"How's the job search coming?"

The question jerked her from her reverie.

"I ran into Chloe yesterday, and she mentioned you had a hot lead on a new job."

"The hot lead fizzled." Emily's lips quirked up in a wry smile. "There was an opening at one of the high schools for a music teacher. I thought I had a real chance, but I got the rejection letter this afternoon."

"That's tough." His gaze turned thoughtful. "Have you looked at any of the private schools in the area? I bet they'd love to have someone with your credentials on staff."

"I haven't, but you're right, they may be more open to someone without a teaching certificate."

"Do you ever regret leaving the symphony?"

For a second, Emily wondered how he knew, then she realized that his sister must have mentioned it to him. "I was honored to play in BSO and to have a leadership role. But being a concertmaster is demanding. Not only are you expected to attend all rehearsals, both full and sectional, there would be solo passages to prepare for. In addition, there are administrative responsibilities and community-engagement duties."

When Emily paused to take a breath, she realized she'd told him far more than necessary. She'd been showing off her knowledge, after diving deep into what being a concertmaster meant. She gave a little laugh. "That's the long answer. The short one is no, I don't regret leaving."

Though she could see he didn't fully understand the why of it, he nodded, then changed the subject again. "So the job hunt hit a snag, but what about moving out of the Oasis?"

"Let's just say, if you see me sleeping on a park bench soon, be sure to stop and say hello."

His eyes widened. "Surely your situation isn't as dire as all that."

Emily's phone buzzed, a jarring sound that she'd meant to change, but hadn't yet taken the time. Pulling the phone from her bag, she quickly scanned the text, replied, then slipped the phone back into her purse.

Seeing the curiosity in Dalton's eyes, Emily answered his question without making him ask.

"Chloe just wanted to make sure I'm really okay with taking an Uber home."

"What did you tell her?"

"I told her I really am fine with it."

"Would you be okay with me driving you back to the hotel?"

"That would be nice, but I'm not ready to leave yet, so if you are, I—"

"I'm not ready to go either."

After grabbing a quick bite to eat at an open-air hut serving a variety of seafood dishes, they went straight for the games of chance. Despite knowing the games were rigged, they had fun trying to pop balloons with darts, tossing rings onto bottles and even playing a version of Whac-A-Mole.

"I'm glad we didn't win." Emily laughed when they came up short—again—on the last game. "There's no space in my hotel room for a teddy bear that's taller than me. And I'm definitely not sharing my park bench with a bear."

By the time they left the fair, Emily was in high spirits, and Dalton appeared content to let her do most of the talking on the drive back to the hotel. Instead of pulling into the loading zone, he snagged a spot on the street.

When she reached for the door handle, his hand on her arm had her turning back, her heart leaping to her throat. Was he going to kiss her?

She licked her lips. "Wh-what is it?"

His gaze searched hers. "Answer me honestly. Are you really close to being homeless?"

"I have options," Emily began, but Dalton's direct gaze had her hesitating. "Okay, nothing firm, but I did respond to an ad from a girl who said she'll have a room coming up soon—a share in a house with five other girls. The downside is it's kind of far away with no place to park, but I don't have a car anyway. Plus, I've never lived with a big group of girls, and it sounds like it could be fun."

"I think I may have an alternative for you to consider."

"Tell me." Emily didn't bother to hide her eagerness.

"I know someone who would be a fantastic roommate. There are a few particular rules to follow, but the house is big and beautiful. Best of all, you wouldn't have to pay a dime in rent."

Emily rested her head back against the settee. Ignoring the glass of red wine she'd poured when she'd reached her room, she closed her eyes and let her mind drift to Dalton's offer.

Startled, and not knowing what to say even after he'd explained the situation, she had simply said she needed to think about it and had deferred giving him a firm answer. Waiting didn't appear to be an issue as he'd clarified he needed to check with his father to make sure he would be on board with the offer.

Which gave Emily tonight to get her thoughts together.

His grandmother, Myra Edwards, had recently experienced a scary heart episode and was waiting to have a cardiac device implanted.

Though there was household staff around during the day, Myra was alone at night. The family wanted someone in the house from ten p.m. to seven a.m. When Dalton had mentioned that the person could sleep in the adjacent room—they just needed to be available if Myra needed assistance—Emily had nearly asked why one of the family simply didn't stay at the house until the surgery.

Not my business, she'd told herself, swallowing the question.

She knew Myra. Or at least knew who she was. They had never been friends. Myra and her husband, Walt, had run in a more affluent social circle.

Myra was also a good ten years younger than Til had been, which put her in her early eighties. Walt, who'd been Til's age, had passed away last year.

If Dalton's father agreed—and Emily accepted—she could stay in Myra's house without charge, be paid for her time and could use the house as a home base.

The commitment would be for only a month or so, just until Myra had the procedure.

This type of "job" wasn't what Emily had had in mind when starting her new life. Then again, while she was figuring out next steps, she did need a place to live and a way to make money beyond busking.

This would be a stopgap. Not only would sleeping there at night not interfere with her day-to-day, she would be helping a family in need.

Opening her eyes, Emily reached for the wineglass, her decision made. If Dalton got the go-ahead from his father, and they could come to terms on salary, Emily would accept the offer.

Though she knew it was the right decision, Emily felt restless and unable to settle, even after finishing off the glass of wine and getting ready for bed.

She let her mind drift, remembering another time, another county fair. One she'd attended with her best friend, Irene Anderson.

From the time they were small, Irene had been the sister Til had never had and the confidante she'd desperately needed. The two girls had shared their hopes and their dreams with each other. There had not been a single doubt in her mind—or in Irene's—that they would be forever friends.

Then Irene's life had come to an end. Measles had hit Grace-Town hard in the 1940s. For some reason, Til had been spared. Irene passed away on a warm summer day, two days short of her fifteenth birthday.

Til had grieved when her mother died, but Irene's loss had been one she hadn't been certain she would ever recover from. For weeks, all she'd done was cry. Her father, an understanding man, had let her grieve, but finally he'd had enough.

He'd told her he loved her, but she needed to get back to living.

The only reason she'd been able to do as he'd asked was because of the letters she'd written, and would continue to write, to Irene after her friend's passing.

In those letters, she'd poured out her heart.

Even after the sharp pain in her heart had receded, she had continued to write to Irene, confiding things she never told anyone else.

Problems that had troubled her were put down on the page. It was funny, but despite the one-way fashion of the letter-writing, she felt as if Irene read every word. That had brought her comfort.

She'd kept the letters in the bottom drawer of her dresser.

As the years had passed, she'd written fewer and fewer letters, dwindling to one or two a year. The mere act of writing to her dear friend had continued to settle her in a way that nothing else had.

Emily thought of the box she'd retrieved when she'd been at the house to get the money in the coffee can. It was filled with letters so deeply personal she hadn't been able to leave them behind.

Taking a deep breath, she retrieved it from the dresser. The first letter she opened had been written after her first date with Vincent.

I went on my very first date ever tonight. Vince took me to see a movie at the Bijou and then to dinner at Seafood Sammy's. I felt awkward at the beginning of the evening, but Vince was so kind...

Reading the details of the date had Emily's lips curving as the night came flooding back. When he'd taken her home that night and walked her to the door, Vince hadn't kissed her, though the look in his eyes had said he wanted to.

It was the same look she'd seen in Dalton's eyes this evening.

Emily's heart rate quickened.

Pulling out a piece of paper and pencil, she did what she'd done for so many years when she'd needed a confidante.

Dearest Irene,

Today was very much a roller-coaster ride. It plummeted when I got notice that the local school system turned down my application. Then Chloe invited me to attend the county fair with her and two friends.

I was excited and had high hopes for the evening. While cordial, the three women know each other well. I soon felt very much like a tagalong.

Making new friends—good friends—takes time. That's what I keep telling myself.

I was considering begging off with some excuse and heading back to the hotel when I met up with Dalton Edwards. He's a professor at

Collister College and a gentleman. We broke off from the group, and I had the most incredible evening. I feel he genuinely likes me.

And—I'm trying hard not to squeal right now—he may have a lead on a place I can rent. I should have more details in a few days.

The roller coaster may have hit some valleys on its way to the top of the tracks, but this evening ended at the summit.

I think he wanted to kiss me, Irene. I know I definitely wanted to kiss him.

There's so much more to tell, little details that I know you'd appreciate, but then this would be an essay, not a letter.

I hope you know just how much I wish you were here with me so we could talk and laugh like we used to.

Please know you are always in my thoughts.

Your bosom friend,

Til

∾

The next afternoon, Emily sat across from Ken Edwards in his downtown office. The building housing his office, which specialized in real estate law, was a short walk from the hotel.

Dalton had texted Emily that morning that the job was practically hers. All she had to do was meet with his dad and get his approval. Since it was the weekend, she was surprised that he'd wanted to meet at his office.

Emily also found it interesting that Ken was the one who had the final say on who would be sleeping in Myra's house, not the woman herself.

Ken leaned slightly forward, his easy smile tempered by the assessing look in his eyes. Emily understood his caution. This was his mother.

After several heartbeats, he spoke. "Dalton tells me that you're new to GraceTown."

"I am." Emily had settled herself in the chair he'd indicated, which left his large mahogany desk between them.

The position of power, she thought, stifling a smile.

He could have easily directed her to several chairs and a love seat grouped for conversation when she'd entered the office, but he'd instead motioned to the visitor chair, then resumed his seat behind the desk.

Perhaps another person might have been cowed by this man with his hand-tailored suit and air of authority. Not her.

Emily remembered all too well the tantrums "little Kenny" had thrown at various community events when he'd been small, behavior that had usually resulted in his parents ordering the nanny to take him home.

Besides, Emily didn't want this job enough to be nervous. If it worked out, she'd do it. If not, she felt sure something better was on the horizon.

"You were in Baltimore prior to coming here."

At Dalton's request, Emily had taken a picture of her résumé and forwarded it to Ken, so he'd had plenty of time to look at it.

"I was," she said. "That information is in the résumé I sent this morning." She smiled and inclined her head. "Did you have a chance to glance at it?"

"I did. I called and verified your tenure with the orchestra. They said it was your choice not to renew your contract." Puzzlement filled his eyes. "They had nothing but positive things to say."

Emily did her best to hide her relief. While she didn't understand how Serena had made that happen, she was grateful. Then again, anyone who could come up with a youth elixir undoubtedly had other tricks at her disposal.

"That's nice to hear."

"What I don't understand is why you quit and why you're in GraceTown now."

Emily lifted a shoulder and let it drop. "I wanted a change. I'm not sure what that change will look like yet, but I was ready for something different."

"And babysitting an old woman appeals to you?"

She wasn't sure which term grated more—*babysitting* or *old woman*. Myra was his mother. In her mind, using such words reeked of disrespect. She ignored the question.

"There are a few things that are still unclear that I'm hoping you can clarify. Dalton indicated I'd be sleeping in Mrs. Edwards's home and would need to be available to tend to her needs during the hours of ten p.m. to seven a.m. During the other hours, there would be household staff around. In addition to free room and board, I would be financially compensated and be able to use the kitchen and other parts of the house during the day."

This last concession was a deal-breaker. Even though it sounded as if she would be here for only a month, Emily wanted a place where she could not only sleep, but live.

"Your use of the house would not include having parties or entertaining friends during your free hours." Ken met her gaze, the warning in his tone coming through loud and clear. "There are many valuable antiques in the home and—"

"I understand," Emily cut in, then immediately regretted the rudeness. "I can assure you that parties aren't my thing. I simply want to make sure that I won't be expected to remain in my room during my free hours."

"Of course."

"Another question. Dalton was unable to tell me the salary for this position." Emily had done her research this morning, calling several area agencies to find out what they charged for a health aide for an overnight shift.

The hourly amount quoted had made her blink. All three agencies had also been quick to inform her that they currently didn't have overnight staff available.

"We would be willing to pay you…"

The figure Ken put out there was half what the agencies

would have charged. While she would have access to the house, she would also be a constant, compared to two or three different caregivers supplied by the agency. Assuming, of course, that the agency could find the staff.

Emily shook her head. "I'm sorry, but that isn't enough for me to make this commitment. I would need…"

The amount she gave him was the amount that had been quoted to her that morning.

Ken feigned a look of shock. "Why, that's—"

"Exactly what any of the agencies in town would charge you," Emily finished for him.

"Their employees are licensed and bonded," he asserted.

"It doesn't take much in the state of Maryland to be licensed as an aide." Emily spoke in a matter-of-fact tone. "Bonded is nice, but so is consistency."

Ken studied her for several heartbeats.

Was that respect she saw in his eyes?

"If I were to agree to that amount, I would need a thirty- day commitment."

Emily nodded. She'd be willing to commit to two months, figuring that it would take at least that long to figure out next steps. "I can do that, as long as Mrs. Edwards is agreeable."

Ken waved off the comment and stood. "We have a deal. I'll draw up the contract. We'll meet at the house tonight and get everything finalized. You can meet my mother and start tomorrow."

Emily pulled to her feet. "Who has been staying with her?"

"Jaclyn. She's done her duty and is ready for it to be over."

The *done her duty* part seemed to indicate that Jaclyn and her grandmother weren't particularly close. Of course, it could simply be a figure of speech.

"I'll see you there at eight." Ken walked to the office door and opened it, effectively ending the interview.

Emily knew where Myra Edwards lived, but the address hadn't been mentioned. Not by Dalton. Or by him.

"I'll be there." Emily stood. "Oh, one thing more."

A watchful look filled Ken's eyes. "What is it?"

She flashed a bright smile. "I need the address."

CHAPTER TWELVE

Emily took an Uber to Myra Edwards's home. When the driver pulled to the curb in front of the three-story Victorian, Emily had to admit she was impressed. Dalton had been right; the house really was gorgeous.

She vaguely recalled seeing pictures of the interior in the *Gazette*'s society section back in the '70s and '80s.

Myra, Heritage League president, and her husband, Walt, GraceTown city councilmember and country club golf committee chair, had always been hosting—or attending—society events. Emily had liked reading the articles about parties held at the couples' home. She'd enjoyed the pictures of the food and décor and searching for names she might recognize.

The only time she'd known anyone had been back in the late '80s when Myra had hosted a garden party reception to honor outstanding community volunteers. Emily had known several of those mentioned in that article.

Emily wondered if Myra's friends from the country club and Heritage League visited her now? Or had they forgotten her as she'd aged and was no longer in the thick of the social scene?

In recent years, Emily had experienced a little of that herself. She knew how it hurt to feel old and useless.

Keeping her focus on the here and now, Emily climbed the steps. Her feet had barely hit the porch when the door opened.

"Emily, welcome." Dalton's gaze shifted to the driver of the silver Toyota pulling away from the curb as he motioned her inside. "Who brought you?"

"Uber driver." Emily waved a careless hand as she stepped into the elegant foyer.

"You should have said you needed a ride. I'd have been happy to pick you up."

"Too late now." Emily kept her tone light. "Besides, I don't have your number."

"That can be easily remedied." Dalton took out his phone. "Take out yours."

When she did, he held his phone close to hers.

"When that screen comes up..." He leaned close, and she inhaled the intoxicating scent of his cologne. "Hit share."

In seconds, he was one of less than a handful of contacts on her phone.

"Success." He grinned, and she couldn't help but smile back as she dropped her phone into her purse.

"I'll take you back to the hotel once we finish here."

"You don't have to do that," Emily protested.

"I can take her." Jaclyn appeared and startled Emily by grasping her arm. She lowered her voice. "You'll be doing me a favor. Otherwise, I'll get stuck hanging with Gran for the rest of the evening. I already have to come back and spend the night."

"I'll let Dad and Gran know you're here." Dalton disappeared down the hall.

"Your father mentioned you've been staying with your grandmother," Emily said to Jaclyn.

Jaclyn made a face. "I drew the short straw. But once you start, I'm free."

"You and your grandmother don't get along?" Emily chose her words carefully, feeling as if she were picking her way barefoot down a garden path strewn with thorns.

"We get along okay, but let's face it, Gran is old as dirt. We have zero in common." As soon as they reached the front parlor, Jaclyn became all smiles. "Gran, I have a friend I'd like you to meet."

Friend seemed a bit presumptuous to Emily. Then again, the simple word inspired confidence, and that was likely Jaclyn's intent.

Emily's heart went out to Myra. She couldn't imagine having such little control over the people having access to her and her home.

Myra sat in a floral wingback chair in the parlor, dressed in a gorgeous pink silk pantsuit. Her dark hair, which had always reminded Emily of polished walnut, was now liberally peppered with gray.

The gaze Myra fixed on Emily was curious. "So you are the young woman who is being foisted upon me in my own home."

Emily met the woman's curious blue eyes. "I would never foist myself on anyone. Whether I stay in your home is up to you."

"Please." Myra waved a hand, reminding Emily of a queen. "Everyone, sit."

Jaclyn took the love seat, while Emily chose one of the chairs.

Dalton's phone buzzed before he could sit. He glanced at the display. "I'm sorry, I need to take this."

He left the room, the phone pressed to his ear.

Ken appeared, a crystal tumbler in one hand, his other holding a small clear cup with several pills. "It's time to take these, Mother."

"If I must." With a resigned sigh, Myra took the pills and the water. After handing the glass back to her son, she refocused on Emily.

"If you agree," Ken said in an easy tone, "Emily will be the one spending nights here."

"If I agree?" Myra arched a brow. "You haven't left me much choice."

Myra's blue eyes, the same vivid shade as her grandchildren's, fixed on Jaclyn. "I want you to know that I've enjoyed every second of my time with you."

Ken slanted a glance at his daughter.

"I've enjoyed it, too. And I'm going to miss our late-night talks." Jaclyn gave a little laugh. "But you're likely better off without me. We all know I'm no good in a crisis."

"Crisis?" The word had Emily turning to Jaclyn.

"Gran has a heart condition. Surely Dad explained it to you—"

"If Emily and your grandmother come to an agreement, I'll explain about the AED and how to use it." Ken tossed the acronym out there with a dismissive wave of his hand. "Though I'm sure using it won't be necessary."

Emily knew all about automated external defibrillators, or AEDs. When she'd tutored at the detention center, she'd helped fundraise for one after an incarcerated young man had gone into sudden cardiac arrest and died.

She shifted her focus to Myra. "Your heart condition is serious."

Myra's gaze never wavered. "There are worse ways to die than to go suddenly."

Emily nodded. She was pretty pleased with how she'd died— painlessly and with no drawn-out illness.

"You're not going anywhere." Ken spoke reassuringly to his mother. "You'll get the surgery and be back to your feisty self in no time."

That brought a slight smile to Myra's lips, a smile that quickly faded.

"Perhaps. I'm still on the fence about the procedure." Shifting her body away from her son and toward Emily, Myra smiled. "Tell me about yourself, Emily."

She felt sure Ken had given his mother all the information he had on her, but accepted that this was Myra seizing control.

Emily understood. As she'd aged, her own control had often been usurped by others intending to be kind and helpful. Everything from the neighbor weeding her garden without being asked, to being told not to bring a dish to the church potluck because *it's a lot of work for someone your age*, to strangers treating her as if she were deaf or blind, or both.

All considerate and well-intentioned gestures. All possessing an undertone that said, *You're old, and we need to take care of you.* For an independent woman, which was what she—and Myra—had been all their lives, it had been a difficult pill to swallow.

Emily relayed the information on her résumé.

When she finished, Myra fixed bright blue eyes on her. "Why would such an accomplished young woman like yourself want to be a nursemaid to a sick old woman?"

"You're not old. Haven't you heard?" Emily kept her tone light and teasing. "Eighty is the new sixty."

Myra offered what could be described only as a snort.

Emily smiled. "As your son likely informed you, I'm figuring out what I want to do with my life. Being here would allow me to figure out next steps."

"Shouldn't you have figured out what you wanted before you invested all that time and education on a career you've abandoned?"

"I view life as a journey," Emily explained. "For some, music can be their entire life. It wasn't enough for me. But all my experiences will forever be with me as I navigate life's byways."

"You're quite the philosopher." Myra's dry tone indicated she wasn't sure that was a good thing.

"In a way, aren't we all?" Emily thought back to all the twists and turns she'd experienced in her ninety-two years. "While your journey has been different than mine, it's shaped you. Spending this month in your home will likely change us both. I believe you and I will learn from each other and be better for this month together."

"Month?" Myra shot a sharp glance at her son.

"By then, I'm hoping you'll have had the surgery—" Ken began.

"I haven't yet decided what I'm doing. Or when." Myra's jaw set in a hard line. "Once I make that final decision, I'll let you know."

"Well, Emily guaranteed she can be with us for a month," Ken explained. "By that time, we'll know more and can proceed accordingly."

"That sounds fair, Gran." Jaclyn rose and surprised Emily by moving to her grandmother's side, crouching down and taking her hand. "For now, we just want you to be safe. You being alone in this big, old house at night worries all of us. If you fall, or if something else happens, who knows how long you could lie there?"

As soon as she returned to the Oasis that evening, Emily notified the desk clerk that she would be leaving tomorrow, a day earlier than planned. When she stopped at the desk the next morning, Chloe was there with a check refunding the charge for one night.

"You don't have to do this," Emily said as Chloe slid the check across the counter.

"You've been the perfect guest." Chloe offered a warm smile. "Having the discretion to do these kinds of refunds is one of the nicest things about managing a small boutique hotel."

Taking the check, Emily slid it into her purse.

"Jaclyn told me you're moving into her grandmother's home."

Was that hurt she heard in Chloe's voice? "I wanted to tell you myself, but our paths didn't cross yesterday."

"I spent the day with Bradley. We went to Baltimore and took in a baseball game."

"Sounds like fun."

"It was."

Emily reached down for her suitcase. "Well, I better—"

"Emily."

Emily straightened to find Chloe rounding the counter.

"I'm sorry about the fair." Clouds filled Chloe's amber eyes. "I realized later that we kind of ditched you for the guys. I'm sorry. It wasn't right."

"It was okay—"

"No." Chloe held up a hand. "Even before the guys showed up, we, well, we didn't include you. Trust me, it wasn't deliberate, just thoughtless. That doesn't make it okay."

"Dalton and I had a nice time." Emily kept her tone light. "All's well that ends well and all that."

"I'm glad you enjoyed yourself." Chloe met her gaze. "But I want to make it up to you."

"You don't have to—"

"How were you planning to get your bike and suitcases to Mrs. Edwards's house?"

"Uber. Speaking of which." Emily pulled out her phone to order one.

"My RAV4 is parked in the back. Let me take you and your stuff over there."

"You're working."

"I'm the boss, remember?" Chloe smiled. "I'm entitled to breaks."

Emily hesitated. "Friday night was fine. You don't owe me—"

Chloe's hand on her arm stopped her. "Please, Emily. Please let me do this."

Fifteen minutes later, after Chloe had wheeled Emily's bike up to the side of the house and Emily had removed her suitcase and violin case from the SUV, Emily waved good-bye to her friend. Then she moved into a lovely room on the main floor of the Edwards's mansion. It wasn't actually a mansion, of course, but it was the largest house Emily had ever lived in.

Ken hadn't been joking when he'd said that the house was filled with antiques. Scads of antiques and loads of collectibles. Definitely enough work to keep a full-time housekeeper busy. When Emily learned that Mrs. Fairfax also did the cooking, she was even more impressed.

The bedroom Emily had been assigned had its own sitting area and bathroom. Though the bathroom wasn't original to the house when it was built in the 1890s, she was glad to have a thoroughly modern one at her disposal.

Once her items had been carefully unpacked, Emily found herself contemplating what to do next.

She'd reached the end of the driveway when a BMW convertible with Dalton behind the wheel and the top down pulled up to the curb.

"Have I told you just how much I like this car?" Emily strode to the passenger side and leaned over. "If you're looking for your grandmother, your father took her to a doctor's appointment. They should be back soon."

"His secretary told me he was here." Dalton's brows pulled together. "She didn't mention him taking Gran to an appointment. My fault." He waved a hand. "I should have texted. Can I give you a lift?"

"Pardon me?"

Dalton flashed a quick smile. "My grandmother says that. It's an old-fashioned response."

Emily shot him a wink. "I'm an old-fashioned girl."

He chuckled. "Can I give you a lift?" he repeated as he gestured with one hand to the violin case. "That looks heavy."

"It isn't—heavy, that is." Emily shifted from one foot to the other. "You don't even know where I'm going."

"Unless it's Baltimore, I have time."

"I'm headed to the town square."

"That's right on my way." Dalton leaned over and pushed the door open. "Hop in."

Setting the case carefully in the back, she fastened her seat belt.

"Emily."

She turned to see Dalton gazing at her with a serious expression. She'd never seen such a look on his handsome face. "I just want to put one thing out there, since it's just you and me right now."

"Okay." Her heart gave a flutter, though she was unable to see where this was headed.

"If you got the impression that we're pushing my grandmother to have this procedure, you'd be right. Since Granddad died in that car accident last year, she's given up. We're not about to let that happen. We're not losing her, too."

Reaching over, she gave his hand a squeeze. "I understand. My father wanted to give up after his stroke, but…"

"You didn't let him."

"No. I didn't." Though Papa's journey hadn't had the happy ending she'd hoped for, she'd had nearly two more years with him.

"I just wanted you to understand where the family is coming from." Dalton pulled the sleek sports car away from the curb, and an upbeat tune about the open road surrounded them.

As she fluffed her hair with her fingers, Emily emitted a happy sigh. This reminded her of the adventure she'd once envisioned. Though the car wasn't yet moving fast enough to create a breeze, she could almost feel the wind in her hair…

At the stop sign, Dalton lightly cleared his throat, and she glanced in his direction to find him staring. "What?"

"You had the strangest look on your face."

"Can I tell you a secret?"

A spark flared in his eyes. "I like secrets."

"Don't get too excited. This will likely seem quite lame to you." She settled herself in the leather seat. "When I was young—ah, younger than now—I was enchanted by convertibles."

"Enchanted, eh?"

She ignored his teasing tone. "I once dreamed about getting into a convertible and heading off down the highway with no particular destination in mind."

"How far did you see yourself going?"

"Far enough to be fun, but not far enough that I couldn't get back before my father discovered I'd left town."

He cocked his head. "Solo?"

Emily inclined her head in question.

"Did you see yourself taking the trip alone or with someone?"

"I guess I never thought that far."

"I vote for with a companion. That would be more fun."

Her noncommittal shrug seemed to amuse him.

They rode in comfortable silence until they drew close to the park, and he stopped the car. "What's the plan?"

"Playing my violin." Anticipation surged as she thought of the Elvis Presley "Can't Help Falling in Love" cover she would debut today. "The music is calling and won't be denied."

"You're ready to seize the day."

Opening the car door, she sprang out. "With both hands."

CHAPTER THIRTEEN

By the time she arrived back at the Edwards's house late Monday afternoon, Emily still hadn't decided what she wanted for dinner. She was leaning toward pizza, but hadn't fully committed to that option.

For now, she would drop off her violin. Then she would either go out or have something delivered.

Intrigued by the voices and laughter coming from the parlor, Emily paused instead of continuing past.

Glancing inside, she saw Dalton and Myra on opposite sides of a game table, playing dominoes. When she started to step back, Myra lifted a hand.

"Come in." Myra motioned to her. "You're not interrupting."

"I was just dropping off my violin and then heading out to grab some dinner." Even as she said the words, Emily realized how rude she sounded. She strolled into the parlor. "Who's winning?"

"I am," Dalton said. "For the moment."

"Mrs. Fairfax will have dinner on the table in thirty minutes," Myra announced. "Though you're under no obligation, you're welcome to join me."

Emily glanced at Dalton. "I wouldn't want to intrude on family time."

Dalton pushed to his feet. "I should have left five minutes ago, but I pulled Gran away from her anagrams by tempting her with a game of dominoes."

"Anagrams?" Emily asked, intrigued.

"I enjoy puzzles, and that's what anagrams are—word puzzles." Myra glanced at a side table that held a pad of paper and what looked like a bunch of scribbles. "I'm old-school. I write down the letters of a word or phrase and then rearrange them to form new words or phrases."

"There are online tools and apps for generating and solving anagrams, but Gran wants nothing to do with them." Dalton offered his grandmother a fond smile. "She likes to do it her way."

"I also enjoy playing dominoes, though at the moment not so much." Myra sighed.

"You can take my place," Dalton said.

"You don't have to leave—"

"I have papers to grade." He offered the excuse to both Emily and his grandmother. "I can stop by Saturday? Unless you have other plans?"

"No need." Myra waved a dismissive hand. "You should be out with your friends on a Saturday night, not babysitting your grandmother."

"I won't be babysitting," Dalton spoke firmly, his gaze now firmly fixed on his grandmother. "I'll be enjoying the company of a woman who can be fun and witty when she's not being a pain."

Myra chuckled. "If you must come over, I suppose I can't stop you."

"Good to see you again," Emily said to him when he turned to leave.

"You, too." He flashed a smile at Myra. "Play fair."

"What's the fun in that?"

He chuckled on his way out of the room.

Myra shook her head, her lips curving. "Grandchildren are simply the best."

"I imagine you're going to miss Jaclyn not being here every night."

"I am." Myra's expression grew serious. "I can't deny I enjoyed having her sleep here. Do you know I stayed up late most evenings so we could chat once she arrived?"

Emily flipped over a domino and moved it into place. Recalling what Jaclyn had said about her grandmother had Emily wondering if Jaclyn had been as eager as Myra for those late-night conversations.

"You may be thinking that Jaclyn is somehow shirking her familial duty by not continuing to stay with me."

Emily looked up from the dominoes in surprise. She'd tried to keep her feelings off her face. Had she somehow given herself away?

"You'd be wrong," Myra continued in a matter-of-fact tone. "Jaclyn has her own life, and I'm extremely proud of all she's achieved. She wanted this job at the Manse, and she went after it."

"It's impressive they'd give a position with such responsibilities to someone so young."

"My granddaughter is an impressive young woman." Myra's eyes shone with pride. "She deserves this time and opportunity to shine."

"I'm sure she's doing a fabulous job for them." Emily played her last tile.

"You won." Myra held out her hand, and when Emily extended hers, they shook. "Good game. Dalton will be pleased that you didn't squander his lead."

Emily cocked her head. "Are you up for another game?"

"You don't need to play if you don't want to."

"I enjoy dominoes," Emily assured her. It was true. When she and her friends hadn't been playing cards, they'd loved playing dominoes or, sometimes, Sequence Dice. "I'm up for another game, unless you're too tired—"

"Not too tired at all." Myra gestured to the violin case. "If you like, I can wait while you take that to your room. I promise not to touch any of the tiles until you get back."

Emily laughed. "I'll hold you to that promise."

In a matter of minutes, Emily returned, dropping into the chair she'd vacated only minutes before.

"Your move," Myra instructed.

Emily lifted a tile with six pips and placed it end to end with another one with six. "Your turn."

They played in silence for several minutes, drawing tiles from the leftover dominoes pile when they were unable to play.

"Mrs. Edwards," Emily began.

"Please, call me Myra." A tiny smile lifted the woman's lips. "If you're going to be asked to potentially save my life, we really should be on a first-name basis."

Emily stilled. "Is your heart condition that serious?"

"That's what the cardiologist tells me." Myra placed a domino with five pips next to another, then motioned to Emily that it was her move.

"Is that why they want you to have the surgery?"

Myra's eyes remained focused on the dominoes. "My doctor wants to implant an ICD, an internal defibrillator."

"Sounds major."

"Major enough." Myra waved a dismissive hand. "Enough about that. I have to admit that I'm curious about where you went with your violin."

"I played in the park." Just saying the words and recalling how good it felt had a smile blossoming on Emily's lips.

Myra cocked her head, a domino poised in her right hand. "Really?"

"This was the first time I played on a Monday. I wasn't sure what to expect, but I attracted quite a crowd." Emily's lips quirked upward.

"How was it?"

"Magnificent. I played a cover of Elvis Presley's 'Can't Help Falling in Love,' and the crowd went wild."

"Walt and I saw Elvis in the late '60s in Las Vegas." Myra's eyes took on a faraway look. "He put on an incredible performance."

Emily watched Myra set down her domino, then she took her turn.

"I believe I'd enjoy hearing you play sometime." A wistful look stole across Myra's face. "Walt and I loved music. All different kinds. Sometimes, when I think back to the times when I held his hand in a concert hall or swayed in his arms on a dance floor, I wish I'd not taken those moments for granted."

"Sounds as if you and Walt had a wonderful life together." Emily recalled how the couple had always been mentioned in the newspaper's society column, back when society columns had been a thing.

"We did." Myra's voice turned as flat as her expression. "He's in a better place, don't you know? That's what everyone says, anyway."

After ninety-two years on this planet, Emily had heard every platitude offered when a loss occurred.

They are in a better place.

You'll see them again one day.

Time heals all wounds.

"My father was my rock. When he passed, I can't tell you how many times I heard that 'everything happens for a reason.'"

Myra sighed. "I've been the recipient of that one as well."

Emily shook her head. "Well, if that's true, I'm still waiting for the reason. He was a good man who worked hard his entire life and was gone too soon."

"My Walt enjoyed a long, happy life." Myra didn't even glance at the dominoes. Her gaze was now focused out the window.

"We'd been married sixty-two years when he passed, but it was still too soon. You say your father was your rock, well, Walt was not only my rock, he was my everything."

Emily expelled a sigh. "I always hoped to find such love. I thought I'd found it, but he didn't stick around."

It was entirely fair to blame Vince for everything, but at the moment, Emily wasn't feeling particularly charitable.

"You're young. You have plenty of time to find the right one."

"For some reason, that platitude isn't any more comforting to me than 'everything happens for a reason.'"

"You know, sometimes, when I lie in bed, I think of Walt and want nothing more than to be with him."

"Is that why you don't want to have the procedure?" Emily spoke softly.

Myra opened her mouth, then shut it.

"How did we get off on this subject?" Myra gave a little laugh. "I believe it's your turn."

On Thursday, Emily decided to head to Maplewood Park to see if any work had been done on the renovation. Actually, it went beyond that. She found herself yearning for the familiar.

Myra was up early, dressed and leaving her room at the same time Emily's feet hit the hallway.

"Good morning." Emily smiled brightly. "Do you have an appointment this morning?"

"I'm going out. Somewhere. I'm not sure where, yet. But I've been spending too much time inside lately." Myra studied Emily's jeans, T-shirt and sneakers. "Where are you headed?"

"I heard there are possible plans to renovate Maplewood Park in honor of that woman who died there." Emily found the words didn't sit right on her tongue. "The civic volunteer."

"Matilda Beemis." Myra gave a nod. "I read about her death in the paper."

"Would you be interested in coming with me to the park? We could check it out together." Emily kept her tone casual and offhand. "Maybe afterward, we could grab a late breakfast?"

"Your shift ended at seven," Myra reminded her. "You don't need to watch over me during the day."

"I didn't plan to watch over you." Emily offered a smile. "Though if you need my help, or I need yours, I hope we'll both be there for one another."

Emily let her gaze scan the park and wondered if she'd gotten so used to seeing it as it was that she'd failed to notice just how run-down it had become.

"Oh my." Myra stared. "I didn't realize there were any parks in GraceTown this shabby."

"The Parks Department budget keeps getting cut." Emily spoke in a matter-of-fact tone, forgetting that, as an outsider, this was something she shouldn't know. "They've tended to focus their efforts on the more affluent areas of town."

"Ken is on the city council." Disappointment filled Myra's voice. "I can't believe he'd condone something like this."

"He may not be aware." Emily decided to give the man the benefit of the doubt. "The budgets are presented, and if there are no objections, they're usually adopted."

Myra shot a sharp glance in Emily's direction. "You seem very knowledgeable."

"I did some investigating when I read that Maplewood might be renovated by volunteers." Emily shifted her gaze from Myra to study their surroundings. "There is a lot of work to be done here. That will be expensive."

"Yes." Myra spoke absently, as if raising the funds wasn't of any concern. "Do you know who is spearheading the renovation?"

"Just what I read in the newspaper." Emily chose her words carefully, not wanting to appear too knowledgeable. "The article said something about a group of Miss Beemis's friends getting together to do it."

"I was involved in a renovation at Funland," Myra admitted.

Funland had been a thriving amusement park until it had shut down in the 1960s. Emily had fond memories of going there as both a child and a young woman.

Emily opened her mouth to comment, but Myra continued before she had a chance. "Our project wasn't a city park, but the considerations would be similar. I have a good understanding of the steps that need to take place."

"Perhaps you could help Matilda's friends," Emily suggested. "You know, lend them your expertise."

"Oh, my dear," Myra waved a dismissive hand, "that was ages ago."

"Doesn't mean your experience isn't still valid."

Emily might have said more, but Myra had gotten that bulldog look, so she let the subject drop.

"I guess what they'll do first is start clearing out the trash and junk," Emily mused, taking note where someone had dumped several large black garbage bags. "The equipment clearly needs to be replaced. Merry-go-rounds like this one may be a hit with kids, but they aren't safe."

"They need to start by formulating a vision and goals."

Myra must have seen the question in her eyes, because she added, "You always start with a vision for the renovation. Then you determine what improvements or changes you want to make and figure out how they align with community needs and interests."

Healthy color was in Myra's face, and the fire in her eyes now hadn't been there earlier. Emily wondered if becoming more involved in the community again was just what Myra needed.

"We could haul off some of this trash," Emily suggested, then glanced back at Myra's Town Car. "But I'm not sure if you want it in your trunk."

Myra shook her head. "I'll take care of it."

Emily smiled to herself as Myra pulled out her phone and made a call.

CHAPTER FOURTEEN

When Saturday rolled around, Emily realized she hadn't heard from Chloe all week. She briefly considered calling her, but knew that calling would be considered rude and a violation of the younger generation's idea of telephone etiquette. Instead, Emily sent a text.

have any plans today?

As a former teacher, Emily resisted the almost overwhelming urge to capitalize the first letter.

The response came swiftly.

J and I are playing tennis at the club—come with?

I don't want to be in the way

U won't

After a few more back-and-forth texts, it was decided that Emily would bike over to Chloe and Jaclyn's apartment, and they'd all go to the club from there. She wasn't sure what club they were going to, but it didn't matter.

Emily had played tennis before, but that had been a lifetime ago. Not certain what to wear, she settled on navy shorts with a striped tee and sneakers.

Jaclyn and Chloe's apartment ended up being a twenty-minute bike ride away. Because of the heat, a light sheen of perspiration covered her skin as she took the stairs to the second-floor apartment.

Chloe opened the door on the second knock. Looking cool and ready to hit the courts in a white tennis dress, she motioned Emily inside. "Come in. We're nearly ready to leave."

Emily stepped inside the spacious apartment that she swore had more square footage than her former house. "This is lovely."

Jaclyn appeared from down the hall and came to an abrupt stop at the sight of Emily. Her gaze dropped to the floor before returning to Emily's face. "I don't see a bag. Where are your clothes? Your shoes?"

"Ah, I'm dressed."

Jaclyn exchanged a look with Chloe.

Whatever was in that look had Emily shifting uneasily from one foot to the other. "Is there something wrong with what I'm wearing?"

"Not exactly," Chloe began.

"The GraceTown Country Club has a tennis dress code." Jaclyn spoke in a matter-of-fact tone. "You won't be allowed on the court dressed like that."

"I'm sorry." Chloe placed a hand on Emily's arm. "I didn't even think to mention the dress code."

Shoving aside her disappointment, Emily shrugged. "That's okay. I—"

"I may have some clothes you can borrow." Jaclyn eyed her with a critical look. "We're about the same size. What size shoe do you wear?"

"Eight."

"Good. Perfect. Same as me. I'll add the clothing and shoes to my bag." Jaclyn started toward what Emily assumed was her bedroom, then abruptly turned back. "It's not a dress, but a tennis skirt and top."

"That's fine with me," Emily said quickly. "Thank you."

Nodding, Jaclyn disappeared down the hall.

"This is really nice of her."

Chloe lowered her voice. "She feels bad about dissing you last Friday, too."

Emily didn't want either of them to feel bad. Spending the rest of Friday evening with Dalton had worked out just fine for her.

"Chloe mentioned you're going solo in the apartment once she moves out," Emily said to Jaclyn on the drive to the country club when conversation momentarily lagged.

From the back seat, Emily saw Jaclyn's shoulders stiffen. Emily laughed and added, "I'm not angling for an invitation to move in, I promise. I'm just curious why you don't want a roommate."

"I like space and I like quiet. That's why I'm not looking to replace her."

"Besides, we both know I'm pretty much irreplaceable," Chloe teased.

Jaclyn chuckled. "Truer words."

Chloe turned in her seat. "How are you liking your new space?"

"Very much." Emily smiled. "It's temporary, but I'm settling in. Myra—Mrs. Edwards—and I are getting better acquainted. The other day, we went to Maplewood Park together, then enjoyed a late breakfast."

Emily felt a sudden chill. She'd thought Jaclyn would be happy that she and her grandmother were building a relationship.

Once they were out of the vehicle and headed to the clubhouse, Emily turned to Jaclyn. "Is everything okay? You seemed to get a little upset when I mentioned spending time with your grandmother. Your dad did hire me to be her companion and—"

· · ·

"My father hired you to be there at night in case anything goes wrong. He didn't hire you to put her at extra risk." Jaclyn stopped walking, and her blue eyes turned frosty.

Emily blinked. "Risk?"

"Gran shouldn't be going out, especially to some dingy park."

"She wanted—" Emily began.

"I don't care what she wants," Jaclyn snapped, then visibly reined in her emotions. "I mean, I do care what she wants—of course I do. However, right now her health and keeping her safe until she has the procedure are my primary concerns."

"While I understand—"

"You don't understand. If you did, you wouldn't have taken her out." Jaclyn's hands clenched into fists at her sides. "You just met her. You haven't sat with her doctors while they expressed their concerns."

Emily said nothing.

"Did you even take the AED with you?"

"What?" Emily asked, startled by the question.

"Obviously, you didn't." Jaclyn blew out a breath. "It should be within easy reach at all times."

"I'll remind Myra of that, if I'm around when she leaves the house." While Emily understood Jaclyn's feelings, Myra's granddaughter needed to understand that Myra was an adult, capable of making her own decisions. "I'm there at night, but during the day, the choices she makes are hers. And she chose to go to the park."

"Jaclyn." Chloe's voice, soft and soothing, had them both turning toward her. "Emily is right. I think it's up to the family to speak with your gran."

"You make a good point. Both of you," Jaclyn admitted somewhat grudgingly. "I'm certainly aware how stubborn and headstrong she can be."

Chloe bumped Jaclyn with her elbow. "Just like someone else I know."

Jaclyn laughed. "That remark is going to cost you."

Pretending to shiver, Chloe shot Emily a wink before refocusing on Jaclyn. "Ooh, I'm scared."

"You should both be scared."

Holding the door open, an older man stepped aside so they could enter. "Good morning."

"Good morning, Alfred," Jaclyn said, offering him a bright smile.

"What did she mean by 'that remark is going to cost you'?" Emily whispered as she and Chloe trailed behind Jaclyn into the gorgeous lobby.

"You and I will be playing against her," Chloe said.

Emily pulled her brows together. Two against one? "That doesn't seem fair."

"Tell me about it." Chloe expelled a heavy sigh. "Jaclyn was the state singles champion three years in a row...and that was when she was still in high school."

∼

Emily had applied at three private high schools her first days under Myra's roof. While she hadn't heard a peep from any of them in the week since she'd personally dropped off the applications, she also hadn't received any dreaded "not interested" letters by e-mail.

After purchasing a used amplification system for her violin, she began playing every day over the lunch hour in the shadow of the Angel of GraceTown statue.

The food trucks in the area, the amazing weather and her own talent led to Emily quickly developing a following. Leaving her case open netted her cash that she used to have business cards made.

Those she dispensed freely with lots of smiles.

On Independence Day, she watched the fireworks explode

over Culler Lake by herself. Chloe and Jaclyn had plans with friends in Baltimore, and Mackenna had a date. Ken came over to spend the day with his mother. Emily wasn't sure where Dalton was or what he was doing. She didn't ask.

When Chloe had relocated to Miami after college, she'd mentioned several times how difficult it was to meet new friends. Til, who'd lived in GraceTown her entire life, hadn't fully understood. She'd always had friends surrounding her.

Emily thought of the fish boil that Lisa and her family were hosting on the Fourth that she'd planned to attend, before she'd become Emily. Everyone she knew would be there.

But those friends were no longer hers, and her new friends, like Chloe, Jaclyn and Mackenna, already had social lives without her. She feared she'd always be on the outside looking in.

It didn't help that the date for Rosemary's wedding was fast approaching. Emily found herself fighting pangs of sadness that she wouldn't be there to see her good friend marry.

Then, on Friday, Emily received an email from Jenna Grace, Rosemary's niece, asking if she was available to play her violin during her aunt's wedding reception. Apologizing profusely for the late notice, Jenna explained that the harpist they'd secured months earlier had broken her wrist mountain biking and had had to cancel.

Someone who'd seen Emily play in the park had passed along her business card, along with a glowing recommendation.

Emily couldn't contain her excitement. In two days, she would meet with Jenna and the bride-to-be to discuss song selection.

When she arrived home, Myra was at the dining room table working on anagrams, using the names of people she'd known through the years.

"Give me the name of someone you know. Don't make it an easy one," Myra urged.

"Serena Nordine." The name simply popped out.

"How do you spell that last name?"

"N-O-R-D-I-N-E." At least that was how Emily assumed it was spelled.

"Thank you." Myra glanced at the paper where she'd written it down. "This one won't be easy, but I do enjoy a challenge."

"How does this work, anyway?" Although Emily had heard of anagrams, she wasn't familiar with how solving them worked.

After joining Myra, Emily got several helpful tips, including starting with shorter words, identifying patterns and focusing on vowels and consonants.

Though they worked primarily in silence, Emily enjoyed the mental challenge. She was in high spirits when Jaclyn arrived late that afternoon with Dalton in tow. Ken strolled in a few minutes later, on his phone, talking business.

They'd come for dinner, and Mrs. Fairfax was making a meal that appeared to be a favorite—smoked salmon, roasted potatoes and an orzo lemon salad.

Emily planned to make herself scarce, but Myra insisted she stay and share the meal. Something in the woman's eyes had Emily agreeing. She and Myra were forging a friendship of sorts. Emily would miss their late-night chats when it came time for her to leave.

That time would be here before she knew it. Which meant that Emily needed to renew her efforts to find a place to live. So far, she'd come up empty.

She assured herself, when her confidence waned, that it would all work out. She would find *something*, at least for the short term.

For dinner, Emily donned one of her favorite new dresses. The simple vivid blue was sleeveless and boasted a crisscross back. She twisted her hair up in a messy bun and took extra time with her makeup.

When she came into the parlor, she saw that Dalton and his father both wore dress pants and button-up cotton shirts. Like her, Jaclyn and her grandmother wore dresses.

Things started out well. The food was amazing and the crème brûlée to die for.

They were enjoying drinks in the parlor when Ken brought up the subject no one had discussed during the meal. "I ran into Jim Hobart at the club today. He asked—"

Myra's eyes flashed blue fire. "Stop right there. I have not changed my mind. I have heard everything Dr. Jim Hobart has to say on the matter, and I don't care to hear more."

The silence that descended over the table spoke volumes.

"Not to change the subject," Emily smiled brightly when all eyes shifted to her, "but I may be playing my violin at a wedding reception."

"Wedding?" Jaclyn asked, appearing interested. "Anyone I know?"

"More likely someone your grandmother would know." Emily shifted her gaze to Myra. "Rosemary Woodsen, Jenna Grace's aunt. Or maybe Rosemary is her great-aunt."

Myra waved a hand as if the exact familial connection didn't matter. "While I'm acquainted with the Grace family, I don't believe I've ever met Rosemary."

"I know her." Jaclyn's expression brightened. "The wedding is less than a month away. I've been discussing catering options with Rosemary and Jenna. They're having the wedding and reception in the backyard of the family home, and the Manse is handling the food and beverages. Everything except for the cake. A friend is making that."

Jaclyn turned to her father. "Daniel, Jenna's husband, is related to Fred—"

"Yes," Ken said heartily, embracing the topic change. "I knew Frederick quite well. He was a good friend of my father's."

A sudden silence fell over the table.

"Yes," Myra said. "Fred and Walt were close friends."

That fact didn't surprise Emily, as the two families ran in the same social circle.

"If the wedding is coming up that soon, why are they only asking you now?" Two lines formed between Myra's brows. "I'd have thought this would have been lined up months ago."

Emily explained about the harpist's cancellation. "Someone whose opinion they trust heard me play in the square and gave my card to Jenna. She called. I'm meeting with her and Rosemary on Sunday to go over song selection."

Myra tapped a finger against her lips. "That's not much notice."

"It'll be fine." Emily would make it work. Just knowing she would be there to see her friend marry—well, that would be a gift.

"When I was younger, I attended so many weddings." A soft look filled Myra's eyes. "Afterward, my friends and I would discuss what we liked about the dresses, the music, even the food."

"My friends and I do that, too, Gran. Some of these dresses are god-awful." Jaclyn made a face. "And don't get me started on food choices—"

"We were never mean-spirited," Myra interrupted. "Well, except for Louella Hooper, who reveled in finding fault. No, it was more talking about what colors and styles we liked...and food preferences. My favorite part to discuss was the vows. Though, back then, they were fairly standard."

"Do you remember the last wedding you attended, Gran?" Dalton asked, speaking for the first time since the wedding discussion began.

"Most certainly. It was the wedding of Louella's youngest granddaughter, Esme. That was at least three years ago, maybe four."

"I remember it being a huge affair." Jaclyn brightened. "Top-of-the-line everything."

"It was." As if tired of the wedding talk, Myra turned to her grandson. "How are things going at Collister?"

"They're going well." Dalton settled back in his seat and took a sip of brandy. "I've got a good group of students in my summer course, a couple who may be interested in pursuing economics as a career."

"Has Joe pulled you over to the dark side yet?" Jaclyn asked, a twinkle in her eyes.

Myra frowned. "Dark side?"

Dalton shook his head. "Ignore her, Gran."

"I want to know what she's talking about," Myra insisted. She gave her granddaughter a look that Emily had learned in her short time in the home meant the heels were dug in.

"I'd like to know, too." Ken lifted a crystal tumbler to his lips. "Sounds intriguing."

Emily said nothing. She knew exactly where this was headed.

"Joe is a professor of folklore studies." Dalton stopped there.

Emily could have told him that that little bit wouldn't be nearly enough to satisfy his grandmother.

Jaclyn laughed. "Which means Joe Wexman believes in all that woo-woo stuff."

"You don't?" Emily wasn't sure what got into her. There was no reason for her to jump into this discussion and so many reasons for her to stay out of it.

"We talked about this," Jaclyn reminded her. "Sedona-like I can handle, but not unexplainable events."

Conscious that she and Jaclyn had captured everyone's attention, Emily simply shrugged.

"I'm with you, Jaclyn." Dalton spoke in a decisive tone.

Ken nodded and took another drink. "I'm not so certain."

Myra's comment had her son snorting.

"Seriously, Mother?"

"When you've lived as long as I have, you come across things that can't be fully explained."

Jaclyn arched a brow. "Such as?"

"Magical healing, for one. One of the women at the club was diagnosed with leukemia and given a very poor prognosis." Myra shifted her gaze, and Emily could see she was looking back. "Sandra told me in confidence that when she was in the hospital, a worker who she'd never seen before—and never saw again— took her hands in hers late one night, and she felt this surge of energy. The next day, her laboratory reports were normal."

"If we're speaking about Sandra Vott, she'd been receiving treatment from the top specialists in the country," Ken said pointedly.

"Yes, but none of the treatments worked," Myra insisted. "When she was admitted to the hospital in GraceTown, she wasn't expected to live more than a few more days."

"Undoubtedly, all the drugs and treatments finally kicked in," Ken said.

"Believe what you want," Myra told her son.

"I suppose you believe all that Angel of GraceTown stuff, too." Without waiting for her grandmother's response, Jaclyn turned to Emily. "What do you think? You play in her shadow every day."

Emily knew all about the angel, but only inclined her head.

"She's talking about this woman who came to GraceTown during the Spanish influenza outbreak and nursed the sick," Dalton explained.

"I read the inscription on the statue." Emily smiled. "So sweet."

"There are some people who think she was some supernatural being." Jaclyn rolled her eyes, making her feelings about the settlement clear.

"Because she didn't get sick?" Emily kept her voice even.

"How she showed up out of nowhere, cared for the sick, then vanished," Jaclyn added.

"Scoff all you want," Myra waved a dismissive hand. "Believe me when I say the longer you live, the more you'll run across things that simply can't be explained."

CHAPTER FIFTEEN

Myra offered Emily her Lincoln Town Car for her meeting with Jenna and Rosemary. The car, still as pristine as it had been when the woman had purchased it in 2011, was a vehicle Myra loved. Which was why Emily assured the older woman that she could bike over to Jenna's house. Still, Myra had insisted.

Emily had to admit as she parked the car in front of the massive three-story brick and stone Victorian that she appreciated both the gesture and the air conditioning. The day that had started out lovely had turned unseasonably hot.

Lifting her violin case from the passenger seat, Emily wiped suddenly sweaty palms against her dress. She wasn't sure why she was so on edge.

She knew—and liked—both Jenna and Rosemary, but there was no chance they'd recognize her as Til.

In her heart, Emily knew it wasn't her friends recognizing her that worried her. She looked totally different—from her age and hair and eye colors, to the five extra inches of height. Not only that, her facial features were different. It was almost as if Serena had known about the blond actress whose strikingly beautiful looks Emily had so admired as a young teen and had given her that face.

No, having her friends recognize her wasn't the issue. It was that she knew *them* and missed them both so much. She hoped she'd be able to keep her emotions under control.

Twenty minutes later, Emily began to relax. They'd had lemonade and sugar cookies at the small table in the kitchen. No pretense, nothing fancy, just taking time to become better acquainted.

Most of the discussion so far had involved Rosemary telling her about her courtship with Barry Whitehead. Though it was old news to Emily, she liked seeing the sparkle in Rosemary's eyes and hearing her vision for the wedding.

"Our vision is to have a simple, but lovely, wedding, surrounded by friends and family."

That comment had Emily recalling her time at the park with Myra and smiling.

"I guess 'vision' is a funny word, isn't it?" Rosemary said sheepishly.

"It's not funny at all. It's lovely. And I promise that if you hire me, I will do my best to make your vision a reality." Emily spoke quickly, wanting them to know her smile hadn't had anything to do with the wedding or reception plans. "The reason I smiled is that the word 'vision' doesn't often come up, and yet, this is the second time I've heard it recently."

"Are you playing at another wedding? I guess most brides have a unique vision for their special day." Jenna's large brown eyes focused on Emily.

"I'm sure they do, but this had nothing to do with a wedding." Emily smiled again. "Myra Edwards and I stopped by Maplewood Park recently. We'd heard there might be some renovations coming, and we were curious exactly how much work the park needed."

"It needs a lot," Rosemary said with a rueful smile.

"I agree with you there. The committee came up. I said the first goal should be cleanup. Myra disagreed. She said the committee needed to formulate a vision, then determine what improvements or changes are desired and see how they align with community needs and interests," Emily explained.

Surprise flickered across Rosemary's face. "Those are really good points."

Jenna set down her glass of lemonade. "Sounds like Mrs. Edwards has been involved in a park renovation before."

"Not a park, but a project involving a building on the grounds of Funland," Emily said.

Rosemary and Jenna exchanged glances.

"She might be someone we should ask to join us when we gather to discuss the project," Jenna said to Rosemary.

"I agree." Rosemary turned to Emily. "Can you give me her contact information?"

"I'd be happy to." Sensing the subject was about to return to the wedding, Emily spoke quickly. "Just for the record, I'd like to help, too."

"May I ask why?" Confusion furrowed Rosemary's brow. "Did you know Til?"

"I want to help because I can understand wanting to honor a friend."

Tears welled in Rosemary's eyes.

With great effort Emily kept her tone even. "And working to better the community. That park really needs work."

Rosemary chuckled. "It really does."

"We'd love your help," Jenna said, then sighed and glanced down at the sheet in front of her. "For now, let's get back to the reception."

"I'm sorry. I should have kept to business."

"Don't apologize." Jenna placed a gentle hand on Emily's arm. "You're very easy to talk with."

Rosemary smiled. "Having you as a part of the reception seems meant to be."

"Though we trust Annie's recommendation, before we lock things down," Jenna's gaze dropped to the list in front of her before returning to Emily, "would you mind playing a few of the tunes on Rosemary's list?"

"I'd be happy to." Pushing back from the table, Emily picked up the case, then opened it, taking out the violin. Once she'd made sure the shoulder pad and chin rest were in the proper positions, she added rosin to the bow. "I also have a few suggestions that I think you might like."

Rosemary leaned forward and clasped her hands together. "I can't wait to hear you play."

Emily started off with Bach's "Air on the G String," one of the pieces on Rosemary's list. She agreed the serene composition was a lovely choice for background music.

The smiles on the two women when the piece drew to a close had Emily moving on to Tchaikovsky's "Waltz" from *Swan Lake*.

The women clapped when she finished.

"May I try one that's not on the list?" Emily asked.

"Yes." The two spoke at the same time.

Fauré's "Pavane" was a graceful piece that Emily believed could create the perfect ambience for a garden reception.

She played the piece from memory, and the romantic essence wrapped around her and squeezed her heart.

When she finished, Emily lowered her violin.

"You are an amazing talent." Rosemary breathed the words. "I'd be honored to have you play at my reception."

"I've never been much of a violin fan," Jenna admitted. "But I am now."

"Thank you."

"So, will you play at my reception?" Rosemary asked, a hopeful gleam in her eyes.

"I'd love to." Gazing into Rosemary's deep-set blue eyes, Emily experienced a surge of warmth. "You're going to be a beautiful bride."

Rosemary stared at Emily, and for a second, Emily swore she wasn't the only one who felt the connection. Then the older woman smiled. "I'm very happy you're going to be there to share my special day."

～

After leaving Jenna and Rosemary's home, Emily couldn't stop smiling. Talking with the two women in such a relaxed atmosphere had been what she'd dreamed of. She hadn't been certain exactly how to renew their acquaintance. Her musical prowess had allowed her to gain access to them.

It also appeared she might be able to help with the Maplewood Park renovation.

For a second, Emily wondered if that's why Serena had blessed her with not only a do-over of her life, but with the gift of music.

No, she decided as she slipped behind the wheel of the Town Car, it must have just happened that way. After all, how could Serena have known that all this would fall into place as it had?

When she parked the car in the garage at Myra's house and handed the keys to Mrs. Fairfax, she learned that Ken had arrived a half hour earlier and taken his mother out for dinner.

Though Mrs. Fairfax offered to make her something if she was hungry, Emily declined. She had the entire evening open, and she was going to seize the moment.

No matter how enjoyable, today had been all about work.

Tonight, she was going to do something fun. Just for herself.

Emily texted Chloe and Jaclyn. When she got no response, she texted Mackenna, who replied that she already had plans.

Emily considered her options. She could go to a movie. She

could grab a coffee or dinner at one of the bistros on the River Walk. She could relax in her room and read.

So many possibilities, but nothing sounded intriguing.

Perhaps if she freshened up and got ready to go out, something would come to her.

After a long, leisurely shower, Emily curled her hair and redid her makeup. Though she had several new dresses calling her name, she chose instead a pair of shorts and a tiny tee that made her feel young and vibrant.

Satisfied with her appearance, she took off on her bike in the direction of the River Walk. She would keep an open mind and knew that something would catch her eye.

That something was booths set up in the town square. The fact that ARTistry in the Park—one of her favorite summer events—started today had totally slipped her mind.

In addition to artists selling fine art, there was photography, handcrafted jewelry and glass art. The food trucks were out in force, as they always were at events that drew these kinds of crowds. The energy in the air wrapped around Emily and told her this was where she needed to be.

After securing her bike to an inverted-U rack, she strolled from tent to tent, inspecting framed photographs of local landscapes and people, functional and decorative pottery items and handblown glassware.

She inhaled the enticing scent of a number of soaps before buying two bars and slipping them into her new backpack. Then she returned to one of the photography tents.

Images captured from old GraceTown caught her eye and had her lingering, flipping through photograph after photograph.

Telling herself to focus on the future, not the past, didn't work. Going through these vintage photos was like taking a trip into her past. She admired photographs of Funland, a car dealership no longer in business and—her heart gave a solid thump—her father's hotel, the Magnolia.

Emily's fingers tightened around the photograph encased in a clear plastic sleeve. She didn't possess any photographs of the hotel that had burned down several years after her father died. Even if she had, they would have been in her house with the other remnants of her previous life.

With fingers that trembled, Emily removed the photograph from the plastic sleeve. The two-story, ten-room hotel, originally built in the late 1800s, had had an elegant and grand appearance.

With its tall, narrow windows, elaborate cornices and low-pitched roof, the brick structure was representative of the Italianate style of Victorian architecture.

Her father hadn't been the first owner, of course, but her earliest memories were of "working" alongside him and her mother. After her mother had passed away, she'd done what she could to help him out.

Emily barely recalled the rocky times during the Great Depression that her father had spoken of. She mostly recalled the good times during the war years and after, when business had been brisk, and the hotel had thrived.

As she traced the outline of the structure with the tip of her finger, her heart swelled with emotion.

She returned the photo to its sleeve, then held it in one hand as she continued to look through the other photographs, hoping to find another of the hotel, but she came up empty.

After going back to the one of Funland, she took the two photographs and set them on the counter, then handed the money to the older man working the cash register.

"Anything else?" He offered her such a friendly smile that, for an instant, she wondered if he knew her. Then, almost instantly, she realized that was ridiculous.

He was retirement age, and she was, well, young.

"Just these two," Emily told him.

"I don't remember this hotel, but my father does." The older man seemed inclined to talk since there was no one else in line. "I can't recall the name right now, but when I showed him the picture, he pointed out exactly where it used to be on the street. It was right next to where the Bijou is now."

Emily opened her mouth to say his father had it wrong. The Magnolia had been another block down from the Bijou. His father had obviously gotten the hotel confused with another business. She shut her mouth with a snap and simply smiled.

"Would you like these in a sack?" he asked.

"Please."

"What did you buy?"

As if she'd been caught with her hand in the cookie jar, Emily felt her heart jump at the familiar male voice. "Just a couple of old photographs."

She turned and saw Dalton standing beside Joe Wexman.

"My wife and I love old photographs." Interest sparked in Joe's brown eyes. "What are they of?"

Emily lifted the plastic sleeves from the sack and held them out. "One is of Funland, and the other is an old hotel called the Magnolia."

"That's it," the older man behind the desk said. "The Magnolia."

Joe studied first one photo, then the other. He lifted his gaze. "You have a thing for vintage hotels?"

"I'm interested in a lot of things," she told him.

"Are the photographs your only purchase so far?" Dalton asked as the three stepped away from the counter to make room for another customer.

"I've been tempted." Emily kept her tone light. "But so far, I've resisted. What about you?"

"I let Sophie do the buying." Joe smiled. "But I'm going to tell her about this booth."

"Where is your wife?" Emily asked.

"She's meeting me by Scoops on the Go in about..." Joe glanced at his watch, and his eyes widened. "Now."

Joe clapped Dalton on the arm and offered Emily a smile. "Great seeing you, Emily. Dalton, see ya, buddy."

When Emily slanted a curious glance at Dalton, he explained, "Joe and I walked over here from campus. Today was the last day of the first summer session."

"You should celebrate."

"Any ideas?"

Emily had a few, but they fled her mind when she spotted Charlie Rogan pushing his mother's wheelchair while Lisa and her daughter-in-law chattered happily.

Though Lisa's MS more often necessitated the use of a cane rather than a wheelchair, Emily knew that when a lot of walking was involved, a wheelchair was usually called into service.

Emily's heart gave a leap as they drew near. It was so incredibly good to see her old friend that she spoke without thinking. "Lisa, it's good to see you."

The greeting had already left her lips when Emily realized her mistake.

A puzzled look furrowed Lisa's brow. "I'm sorry. Have we met?"

With her heart fluttering in her throat like a captured hummingbird, Emily considered, then discarded, various responses, not one of which made the least sense. She felt as if she were drowning, going under for the final time when Hannah spoke.

"Lisa, this is Emily Curtis. She's the one Charlie and I met at Destiny."

The confusion fled Lisa's face. "The one staying with Myra Edwards."

"I am." Emily considered how much to elaborate and decided that the less said, the better.

"It's a pleasure finally putting a face with the name." Lisa shifted her gaze to Dalton. "How is your grandmother doing?"

"She's doing well." Dalton also kept to the basics.

Emily had quickly discovered that the Edwards family preferred to keep their private affairs private.

"I'm glad to hear it."

"It was lovely meeting you," Emily said. "Hopefully, I'll be seeing you all again." Tightening her hold on the small sack, she made her escape.

Under different circumstances, Emily would have loved to stay and talk with Lisa, but seeing the lack of recognition in her friend's eyes tore at her heart.

They'd once been the closest of friends, and now they were strangers. At that moment, Emily realized that deep down she had assumed—hoped—that her friends would somehow know her, somehow sense her essence lurking beneath the different exterior.

But Rosemary hadn't, and neither had Lisa. The realization made Emily want to weep.

She was nearly out of earshot when she heard Lisa say, "She seems like a nice young woman. I could see you and her being friends, Hannah."

Not her and Lisa being friends, but her and Hannah.

She'd been so lucky to have the friends she had, friends who'd kept her active and, well, young at heart.

Emily missed each and every one of them. Despite high hopes, she'd not been able to connect with them in the way she wanted. Which brought her to a hard truth, one she needed to accept— what was lost could not always be regained.

CHAPTER SIXTEEN

Before she'd left her meeting with Rosemary and Jenna, Emily had not only had a contract to play at the wedding reception, but an invitation to the prenuptial dinner held on Friday night.

It was to be a casual event, catered by the Manse, at Daniel and Jenna Grace's home. They'd told Emily she could bring a plus-one.

Chloe was her first choice, but Emily discovered she would be helping Jaclyn with the catering. Mackenna had a date.

Friday rolled around, and Emily still didn't have a plus-one. Though she'd attended many events solo throughout the years, tonight she felt in need of some moral support.

When Myra asked that morning if she'd be interested in sharing a scone and coffee on the back terrace, it wasn't the offer of a lemon blueberry scone that had her saying yes.

Emily lifted the china cup to her lips and peered at Myra over the rim. "What are your plans for this evening?"

Myra broke off a piece of scone. Her lips curved ever so slightly. "This may shock you, but my social calendar is completely open. Why do you ask?"

As age had crept up on her in her previous life, Emily had

discovered she could no longer go out as frequently as she had in the past. Yet she'd also discovered that spending too much time alone and not having a purpose wasn't healthy. Not for her. And, she suspected, not for Myra.

"Tonight, I'm attending a prenuptial dinner at the Grace home." Emily kept her tone deliberately casual. "Rosemary and Jenna said I could bring a plus-one. Would you be interested in going with me?"

Surprise skittered across Myra's face. She lowered her cup, setting it on the saucer. "Now why on earth would you want to take an old woman as your plus-one?"

The hope that eventually Myra could find some friends among these women who'd once been Emily's was something Emily preferred to keep to herself.

"You're poised and possess a vast amount of knowledge about any number of things," Emily said honestly. "As you are a master of small talk, this is the perfect party for you."

Emily could almost see the question hovering on Myra's lips. "I'm also being selfish," Emily added. "It would be fun for me to have someone to go with. You'll likely know most of those in attendance, so you can pave the way for me to become better acquainted."

Myra closed her mouth and took a contemplative sip of coffee. "It might be fun."

Emily fought a surge of hope. "Is that a yes?"

"Yes." Myra smiled. "It sounds like fun."

Emily wore one of her new summer dresses, this one a hot pink fit and flare that she coupled with ballet flats. Though she would have preferred to wear heels, since the party would be in a back-yard, flats seemed more sensible.

Myra emerged from her bedroom shortly before they were to

leave in a casual A-line dress that boasted blue flowers on a white background. Her shoes, the same blue as her dress, had kitten heels. The straw bag she carried held the AED.

They were ready to walk out the door when Dalton appeared.

His gaze shifted from his grandmother to Emily. "Wow. You two look gorgeous. Where are you headed?"

"Emily is taking me as her plus-one to Rosemary Woodsen's prenuptial dinner." Myra waved an airy hand. "It's really more of a garden party. Your sister is overseeing the catering."

Dalton's gaze returned to Emily. "You're taking Gran?"

"I am." Emily smiled at Myra. "We best get going."

When they reached the Grace home, Rosemary and Barry greeted them at the front of the house. "Thank you so much for coming."

Emily saw Rosemary trying to place Myra, while Barry was trying to place Emily, so she quickly performed the introductions, then added, "Thank you both so much for the invitation and for the chance to be part of your big day tomorrow."

"Barry and I have known each other for years." Myra spoke for the first time, offering Rosemary's fiancé a warm smile. "He and I served together on the Funland renovation committee."

"I didn't realize you had that kind of experience." Rosemary glanced at her fiancé.

"This lady is the one with the experience." Barry, a genial fellow with a Vandyke beard, gestured to Myra. "She led the committee."

Interest sparked in Rosemary's blue eyes as they settled on Myra. "You may have heard about the Maplewood Park renovation project. Would you be interested in joining our committee? We could definitely use someone with your expertise."

"I'd be interested in visiting with you about the possibility." Myra offered a warm smile. "For now, please know I wish you both all happiness."

The backyard, the site for tomorrow's nuptials, had been

transformed into a romantic paradise, with flowers and fairy lights and a tempting array of food on long tables covered in linen.

Emily had known that Daniel and Jenna would go all out, especially when she'd heard the Manse was catering tonight, but she hadn't expected this. Instead of heading straight for the food, she and Myra wandered the area, visiting with the other guests.

Emily noticed immediately that the guest list hadn't been confined to the wedding party or even to those, like her, who had a part in the wedding.

Most of those in attendance she knew. The trouble was, they didn't know her.

Geraldine and Beverly, her cardplaying buddies, were there. Beverly, the more social of the two, actually came up to Emily and Myra and introduced herself.

"I've heard that you two are quite the cardplayers," Emily said after the introductions were completed.

"Who did you hear that from?" Geraldine was nobody's fool, and her gaze turned sharp and assessing.

"I-I'm not sure," Emily stammered. "Somewhere."

She should have known that Geraldine would be all over that statement.

"Oh, Geraldine, everyone in GraceTown knows how much we love playing cards." Beverly spoke cheerfully. "I believe it was even mentioned in that article about Til."

"I'm sorry you lost your friend." Emily shifted uncomfortably from one foot to the other.

"I'm sorry as well," Myra added. "Although I didn't know her personally, I read the article in the *Gazette*. She was truly an asset to the community."

"That was our Til." Beverly nearly sighed the words. "She was determined to do what she could to make the lives of those in GraceTown better."

"She was also one heckuva cardplayer," Geraldine added.

"What kind of cards do you play?" Interest sparked in Myra's blue eyes.

As the conversation veered to the virtues of various card games, Emily slipped away. Myra didn't need her hovering around.

It was equally clear to Emily that her old friends saw her as a young woman, a granddaughter type rather than a friend with shared experiences. She couldn't talk with them about the '70s or the '80s, couldn't recount where she was when Kennedy was shot or when Neil Armstrong became the first person to walk on the moon.

No more looking back, she reminded herself.

Out of the corner of her eye, she spotted Chloe at the appetizer table. Pleasure rushed through her. She'd nearly forgotten that Chloe would be here.

With purposeful steps, Emily crossed the yard to where Chloe was replenishing crispy triangles of shrimp toast.

"Looks like Jaclyn is keeping you busy."

The comment had Chloe looking up. "Hi, Emily." Chloe offered a quick smile, then returned her attention to the toast. "Enjoying the party?"

"I am." Lifting a piece of shrimp toast, Emily took a bite and went for casual as she asked, "Are you free on Sunday? I—"

"I'd love to talk, Em, but we're shorthanded, and now I see we're nearly out of crab cakes." Turning, Chloe strode off without a backward glance.

"Those shrimp toasts are amazing."

Emily whirled to see Jenna and Daniel smiling at her. "They are incredibly good."

"Emily, I'd like you to meet my husband." Jenna laid a hand on her handsome husband's arm. "Daniel, this is Emily Curtis."

Daniel, with his mass of brown hair and vivid green eyes, smiled. "It's a pleasure to meet you."

"I love your books." Emily spoke from the heart. She'd

devoured his first two releases and was eagerly anticipating his third.

"Emily Curtis." A contemplative look filled his eyes, then a smile broke free and had the fine lines around his eyes crinkling. He chuckled.

"What is it?" Jenna asked. "What's so funny?"

"Emily Curtis," he repeated. "Curtis is the name of the protagonist in my first novel, and Emily is the name of a prominent secondary character." Daniel shifted his gaze back to Emily. "Good thing I didn't know you back then, or you might think I commandeered your name."

Actually, Emily thought, she was the one who'd done just that. "I would have been honored if that had happened."

Daniel smiled. "After listening to Jenna and Rosemary rave, I can't wait to hear you play tomorrow."

Emily's gaze slid to where Barry and Rosemary chatted with a couple, his hand around her back and resting lightly on her waist. "It's as if her coming to GraceTown and meeting him was meant to be."

"I've had that same thought," Daniel said, then glanced at his wife. "Not just about Rosemary."

The love in his eyes stole Emily's breath.

Would she ever have that? She thought she had found that with Vince. But if he had truly loved her, the way he'd said he had, wouldn't he have understood that she'd needed to take that time to care for her father, a man who'd always been there for her?

Even when Vince had moved to Baltimore for his new job, she'd thought—hoped—that he'd wait for her.

Yet, when her father had passed away less than two years later and she'd looked up Vince, she'd discovered he'd been married for nearly a year.

Emily had told herself it was for the best that she had found out what he was like. Regardless of what he'd said, he hadn't loved her. At least not the way a man should love a woman he planned to marry.

The years that had followed had been rich and full. She'd carved out a life for herself, filling it with projects that had satisfied her and with friends who'd loved and supported her.

Marriage, well, marriage would have been nice, but only to the right man…and he'd never come along.

Perhaps he would never come along in this lifetime either.

Whatever happened, Emily was good with it. She just hoped that even if the prince of her dreams never appeared, she still got to kiss a few frogs along the way.

∿

Emily assumed Myra enjoyed the party, even though she was uncharacteristically quiet on the drive home.

Seeing the fatigue on the older woman's face had Emily not pressing for details. She hoped the party hadn't been too much for her.

When she parked the car in the garage, she hurried around to open Myra's door and give her a hand, but found Myra already standing.

"Thank you for taking me with you." Myra's lips curved up ever so slightly. "It's been a long time since I've had such an enjoyable evening."

"It was fun." Emily walked beside her into the house. "Everyone was so warm and welcoming."

"Beverly invited me to be a substitute for their card group." Myra tossed the words out there as Emily pulled the door shut behind them. "Apparently, with Til's passing and Rosemary's honeymoon, they are in dire need of someone who knows and enjoys cards."

"What did you tell them?"

Myra smiled. "The same thing I said about being on the renovation committee. I would give it some thought and get back to them."

Emily's hopes plummeted. Then she sternly reminded herself that these were Myra's decisions to make, just like the surgery was. "Always good to think things through."

"I'm going to do both, of course."

"What?" Emily couldn't hide her surprise. "You are?"

"I'll wait a few days, then let them know." Myra opened the door to her suite and turned back to Emily. "It's never good to appear too eager."

As the woman disappeared into her room, a thought struck Emily. Had Jaclyn said something to her grandmother about Emily's frequent texts to both her and Chloe asking about getting together?

Had she been too eager and, because of that, pushed them away? It was definitely something to consider.

CHAPTER SEVENTEEN

Since the wedding wasn't until four, Emily had the morning to herself. By seven thirty, she and her bicycle were on the bike path.

She rode until she reached the grounds of the former Funland. There was little left of the vibrant amusement park that had been a popular destination for decades.

There was a nondescript, low-slung building, built in the 1960s, used by Parks & Rec staff. The only other building on the property was the bandstand.

Originally constructed in the garden area of the amusement park, where bushes were trimmed in the shape of mythical creatures and the scent of flowers hung heavy in the air, the bandstand had been revitalized several years back.

Emily vividly recalled coming to Funland with her father shortly after WWII had ended. The park, which had struggled during the Great Depression, had experienced a resurgence when the country had entered the war.

That day, her fourteenth birthday, the sky had been an intense blue, and the sun had shone brightly down upon them. Her father, who'd rarely left the hotel in anyone else's care, had agreed to take her and Irene to the park to celebrate.

Emily recalled entering this section of Funland through white lacquered gates. Those lovely gates were long gone.

Music popular at the time flowed joyfully into the air from a raised platform. A red canopy overhead shielded the swing band from the sun.

Concrete benches on each of the terraced levels looked down on the band and on visitors dancing the Lindy Hop and the jitterbug.

She and Irene had wanted to sit close to the band, but her dad had barely started down the steps when he'd needed to stop. Looking back, Emily realized he'd been experiencing heart issues long before his stroke.

The day was so vivid in her mind that Emily didn't have to close her eyes to see the bandmembers in their fashionable attire —tailored suits with wide lapels, padded shoulders and high-waisted trousers.

There had been a woman in the band, her blond hair accentuated by a floral scarf that brought a pop of color to her knee-length navy dress as she played the violin.

Emily remembered being fascinated by the sounds flowing from the instrument. She hadn't been able to stop raving about the woman's talent. It seemed extra special that the woman looked like Til's favorite movie star. Irene had been more fascinated by the male bandmembers and their trilby hats, which she'd dubbed *dreamy*.

Smiling in remembrance, Emily parked her bike. She noticed the new metal gate leading to the bandstand where small concerts and plays were held was unlocked. Though the mythical bushes and abundance of flowers were gone, the fact that a small part of Funland had been salvaged was a reason to rejoice.

When she'd ridden past, Emily had noticed one vehicle parked by the maintenance building, but so far she hadn't seen another soul. She started down the steps that led to the stage. She was halfway there before realizing she'd been mistaken. She wasn't alone.

And it wasn't a Parks & Rec person sitting on one of the concrete benches, but Sophie Wexman.

Sophie turned to her, the sunglasses she wore hiding her eyes. Her lips curved upward. "It's Emily, isn't it? We didn't get a chance to talk that night at Destiny. I'm Sophie, Sophie Wexman."

"It's good to see you again." Emily gestured widely with one hand. "This was once such a beautiful place."

Then, worried that Sophie might think she was criticizing all the efforts that had gone into making this venue viable, Emily quickly backpedaled. "Not that this isn't nice."

"It's lovely now, but a shell of its former glory."

Emily nodded. "What brings you here today?"

"Remembering someone I once knew." Sophie sighed. "Today was his birthday." Her lips lifted in a slight smile. "A very special man, long gone."

"I had a special man in my life once." Emily spoke haltingly. "I thought he loved me, but when I needed him to wait for me, he —" She stopped. Why in the world had she brought up Vince?

"He couldn't wait?"

"He chose not to," Emily clarified, then clamped her mouth shut.

"I believe everything happens for a reason." Sophie's gaze returned to the stage. "I can't get over how different it is now."

"Because of the metal trusses and canopy," Emily said without thinking. "Instead of red fabric. And no one dances down there anymore."

Sophie's head swiveled toward Emily, and she lowered her glasses. "How do you know that couples used to dance near the band? That was discontinued shortly after WWII."

Emily simply shrugged.

Sophie stood. "Would you go for a walk with me?"

"Sure." Emily followed Sophie up the steps. "Though there's not much to see now."

"Joe mentioned he and Dalton ran into you at the art fair, and you found a photograph of Funland."

"I did. It's of the steeplechase ride." Emily's lips curved upward as she recalled the ride she and Irene had taken that long-ago day. "When you put two riders on that wooden horse, you flew down the track."

Sophie chuckled. "Imagine riding it in a skirt."

Emily shook her head, her lips curving upward. "I can't— imagine it, that is. Though there was a woman in the photograph I purchased wearing a skirt. And a hat with flowers around the brim. I don't know how it stayed on."

"A woman. Really?"

"A man rode behind her."

Sophie stilled. "I'd love to see that photograph."

"I'll make sure you do."

"Thank you. I'd appreciate it."

They strolled aimlessly, stopping in a spot that was now a flat expanse of mostly dirt with patches of grass. If Emily's sense of direction was correct, this was where her father had stopped to buy her and Irene a hot dog, a Coca-Cola and cotton candy.

"No picnic tables," Sophie murmured.

"No lush green grass and flowers." Emily sighed. "And no cotton candy machine."

"Do you know they used to call cotton candy fairy floss?"

"I didn't know that." Emily shook her head. "That must have been a long time ago."

"A very long time," Sophie agreed, then cocked her head. "I never asked what brought you here today."

"I was feeling sorry for myself," Emily admitted. "I, ah, I'm new to GraceTown, and I'm having a difficult time finding a circle of friends."

Sophie offered a sympathetic smile. "It may sound trite, but friendships take time to root and grow and blossom. I believe you'll make new friends, Emily. Friends as good as the ones you left behind."

~

Emily's brief conversation with Sophie eased much of the tension that had gripped her. Or maybe it wasn't even that conversation. Maybe it was the exercise or reliving in her mind those happy times at Funland with Irene and her dad.

She thought about the woman in the swing band playing the violin and smiled. That had likely been her first exposure to the instrument, and look at her now.

When Emily returned home, Myra offered the use of her car for the evening. Emily was backing out of the driveway when Dalton arrived to have dinner and spend the evening with his grandmother.

Dalton had offered to come over so Emily wouldn't have to rush home from the wedding reception. She'd tried to tell him she would for sure be home by ten, but he'd only reiterated there was no need.

There was valet parking in front of the Grace home. Emily had heard Rosemary and Barry had gotten the okay to use the parking lot at SensorTech, a local business.

Emily stepped from the Lincoln and handed the fob to a young woman with a friendly smile.

"This is for you." The young woman handed her a claim ticket. "We'll take good care of your vehicle."

"Thank you. I'd appreciate that." The last thing Emily wanted to do was take the Town Car back with a scratch or dent.

With her violin case in hand, Emily strolled toward the home and around the side to join wedding guests mingling in the backyard.

All of those who'd been there last night were back, along with a large group of new faces, most known to Emily.

There was now a raised dais with an arbor of flowers overhead, where Rosemary and Barry would say their vows. Off to one side of the arbor stood a lemon tree, fruit hanging from its branches.

Emily had lived here for nine decades and never known that lemon trees could not only grow, but thrive, in this climate.

She took the glass of champagne offered and wandered the backyard, wondering what kind of music Rosemary and Barry had chosen for the ceremony. She didn't have to wait long.

"If you could all please take your seats," Daniel announced in a loud voice that filled the area. "It's time."

Though Emily sat in the back, her aisle seat afforded her a perfect view of the ceremony. She still couldn't believe her luck. If she hadn't played the violin, there was no way she'd have had this chance to see her friend marry.

Barry stood at the front, looking handsome in a dark suit. The sounds of "Here Comes the Sun" filled the air and made Emily smile.

A vision in pink lace, Jenna walked to the front with Barry's son. Once Jenna passed her row, Emily turned and caught her first glimpse of Rosemary.

Her friend wore a flowing, boho-style dress with bell sleeves and lace. Embroidered flowers around the neckline added a nice pop of color to the gauzy white dress.

Rosemary's long hair, normally worn in a braid, had been elegantly swept back from her face and adorned with a ring of flowers.

As she watched Rosemary sweep down the aisle, Emily felt her heart swell. She didn't think she'd ever seen her friend look happier.

Rosemary strolled on Daniel's arm down a center aisle strewn with rose petals. The glow on her friend's face when she saw

Barry at the front and their eyes locked brought tears to Emily's eyes.

Amy Rutt, the officiant, a tall woman with kind eyes, smiled when the couple reached the front.

"Thank you all for coming to share this special day with Rosemary and Barry," Amy said. "They have chosen to begin the ceremony with a song that reflects their feelings on this amazing day." The woman turned to her left and motioned for a young woman to begin. "The song will be played and sung by Barry's niece, Lola Whitehead."

Emily couldn't believe her eyes. Lola was the musician from the River Walk, the one who'd refused to busk with her.

When the last strain of "What a Wonderful World" trailed off, Emily couldn't keep from smiling.

The song was the perfect start for the ceremony joining two older people who had started their relationship as friends and love had followed.

Tears filled Emily's eyes when she heard Rosemary say, "I vow to be your confidant, your partner in laughter and your comfort in time of need."

Even more than the words of love the two exchanged, the promise of comfort and laughter touched Emily's heart. It was what she'd wanted with Vincent.

She reminded herself that was the past, and she was no longer going to dwell on that time. She was going to look ahead and embrace all of her blessings.

When the ceremony ended, everyone clapped.

Emily stepped away and picked up her violin. She got the nod from Jenna and began to play.

She caught Lola eyeing her several times during the reception, but remained focused on the music.

The sight of Jenna approaching her had Emily's heart beating faster. Once she finished Fauré's "Pavane," she lowered the violin. "Is everything okay?"

"You've been playing for forty minutes straight. It's time to take a break."

"Thank you, but playing is what I was hired to do."

"You're doing a fine job." Jenna touched her shoulder. "But we want you to enjoy this celebration, too. You may be new to GraceTown, but you're a part of our community now."

The sentiment touched Emily in a way that Jenna could never imagine. Glancing around, she inhaled the sweet scent of flowers as sounds of laughter and conversation wrapped around her.

Today was truly a joy-filled occasion. Though Emily had chosen to wear a "little black dress," the attendees were dressed in every color of the rainbow. The brightness only added to the fun, festive feel.

"Please, take a break. Get yourself something to eat and drink." Jenna studied her for a moment. "Sophie mentioned running into you at Funland earlier today."

"I rode my bike out there this morning." Emily kept her tone light. "Fresh air and exercise. Nothing like it."

"Sophie said you're very knowledgeable about Funland."

"Not really. I—"

"Violet is another person who has a knack for knowing things that surprise us." Jenna stared at Emily expectantly.

Emily nodded. She knew Violet. Jenna's younger sister had come with her to GraceTown. She'd left to take a gap year before college. She hadn't been back.

A person new to town would likely ask for clarification on who Violet was, but Emily didn't want to prolong this conversation, so she said nothing.

Jenna laid a hand on her arm. "Well, thanks again for what you've done to make this day special for Rosemary and Barry."

"It's been a pleasure."

When Jenna left to mingle, Emily decided to use this short break to convey her congratulations to Rosemary and Barry. She waited, then approached the happy couple once they were finally alone.

Rosemary noticed her approach and smiled. "Thank you for the lovely music. You play beautifully."

"I'm so happy for you. You deserve only the best." To her horror, Emily heard her voice crack. She hastily cleared her throat.

Rosemary didn't appear to notice. She linked her arm with Barry's and smiled up at him. "This one is definitely a keeper."

"Well, best wishes to you both." Keeping a tight hold on her rioting emotions, Emily turned to Barry. "You're a lucky man."

Barry chuckled. "Don't I know it."

When Emily saw several of Barry's relatives approaching, she made her exit and headed to the refreshment table.

"Club soda," she told the young man. "With lime."

"That's how I like it, too."

Emily turned and found herself face-to-face with Lola.

"You're Emily, right?" Lola extended her hand. "Lola."

"The song and arrangement were amazing." Emily moved away from the refreshment table.

Lola stepped away with her, sipping her own club soda. She gestured with her glass. "I wondered how this would go down. I mean, I've never attended a wedding of anyone this old."

"Age is just a number when you're in love. Those two are definitely in love."

Lola nodded, then her gaze turned assessing. "You play really well."

Emily sipped her drink. "Thank you."

"Did you find a place to busk?"

"I did." Emily's lips curved. "I play in the town square by the angel statue."

"If you want to join me sometime, I wouldn't say no."

"If you want to join me sometime, I won't say no either." Emily took another long drink. "Well, I best get back to doing what I was hired to do."

On her way back to her violin, she saw Chloe with Jaclyn, laughing and talking. Emily didn't bother to walk over and say hello.

She'd been able to watch Rosemary marry and to congratulate her on her special day. That would have to be enough.

CHAPTER EIGHTEEN

Emily played her violin for the rest of the evening, then drove home. She hadn't been sure how late the event would go, but knowing Dalton was there with Myra, she hadn't worried.

She was back in enough time to start her shift.

Surprisingly, Myra had already retired for the evening.

"Was she feeling okay?" Emily couldn't stop the surge of concern. "She doesn't normally go to bed this early."

"Well, she beat me at Scrabble and told me I was losing my edge." His lips curved. "I'd say she was feeling pretty good."

Emily smiled.

"Can I interest you in a glass of wine?"

"I'd love a glass." Setting down her violin case, Emily turned to get the bottle and a glass, but Dalton motioned her down.

"I'll get it." Setting aside his wineglass, he rose and gestured to the sofa. "Sit. Relax. I'm betting you were on your feet most of the evening."

As a matter of fact, once the reception had begun, Emily hadn't sat down once.

In minutes, she had a glass of red in her hand as she sat on the floral sofa, Dalton in the chair opposite.

"Are you sure your grandmother is okay?"

"She was in an excellent mood. She informed me she's been asked to be a substitute in some card group. And also that she was asked to head the planning committee for the Maplewood Park renovation."

"They're lucky to have her. Because of her work on the renovation at Funland, she has the expertise they need."

"I'm curious." Dalton relaxed against the back of the chair. "How did they discover she has that experience?"

"I mentioned it to them." Emily shrugged. "I had no idea if she'd be interested in taking on such a leadership role, but it appears she is interested. It's a good fit."

"I'm hoping this means she'll have the surgery."

"I hope so, too."

"Enough about Gran." Dalton focused those intense blue eyes on her. "Tell me about your evening. How was the wedding?"

"Beautiful. So lovely." Emily's lips curved. "The reception was amazing, too. The Manse outdid themselves on the food. I saw Jaclyn and Chloe. They were busy, and so was I, so we didn't have a chance to talk."

"Who was there I might know?"

Sipping her wine, Emily considered. "It was mostly an older crowd. The younger guests were ones you'd expect—Joe and Sophie, Hannah and Charlie and, of course, Daniel and Jenna. Dr. Moorhead's son—I believe his name is Sawyer—was there, along with Annie Laggett."

The Laggett family, Emily knew, were longtime friends of the Edwards family.

"That's it?"

"Like I said, it was definitely an older crowd. I didn't fit in." Emily heard the wistfulness in her voice. The truth was, she didn't fit in anywhere. Not anymore. "I told myself that I wasn't there to socialize. I was simply there to do a job."

"Yes, but I hope you had a little fun, too."

Emily nodded absently.

Much of the good feelings she had carried with her from the reception had faded. She realized even if she had been there as a guest, it wouldn't have been the event she'd looked forward to a couple of months earlier with eager anticipation.

"Have you ever thought what you'd do if you had a chance to start over?" The question popped out before she had a chance to pull it back.

Dalton studied her for a long moment. His eyes turned soft.

"That's what you're doing now—starting over." Instead of answering, Dalton had turned the question back to her. "Are you regretting leaving Baltimore and the symphony? Leaving your friends?"

He'd gotten it wrong. So very wrong.

She didn't correct him.

"When I made my choice, I was excited, and okay, a little scared. I wanted to spread my wings and chart my own course. I felt as if my previous choices had never really been my own."

"I can see where being a concertmaster could take over your life and be all-consuming."

A logical assumption, but again, a faulty one.

"The lack of choice started way before the symphony. It began in my childhood when my mother died. I was only nine, and suddenly it was just me and my dad. Choices available to many other kids at the time weren't open to me. My father needed my help. A normal childhood was out of reach." Emily shifted her gaze to the fireplace hearth, cold and dark. She wondered why she'd brought this up.

Because you need someone to talk with, to bounce thoughts off of.

Yet that begged the question, *Why Dalton?*

When she looked into his sympathetic blue eyes, what was murky became clear. This was someone she could trust.

She expelled a shaky breath and tightened her fingers around the stem of her wineglass. "When I was twenty-five, I met someone, and we became engaged. My wedding was fast approaching when my father had a stroke. He needed me. I couldn't abandon him. I don't regret my choice to care for him, even though it cost me a relationship."

"You were a good daughter."

Emily shook her head. "Anyone would have done the same."

"Not anyone," he said softly.

"Yes," she insisted. "At least if their father was like mine."

"You were lucky in that regard."

"I guess I was. But I sometimes wonder what my life would have be like if I hadn't been placed in such circumstances." Emily cleared her throat. "Coming here was to be my new start, my opportunity to finally focus on me, on what I want."

"New starts can be rocky." Dalton twirled the stem of his wineglass between his fingers. "There is one thought that occurs to me."

Trying to ignore the knot forming in the pit of her stomach, Emily set down her glass.

"If you really want to carve out a different kind of life, caring for my grandmother isn't doing that." Dalton's gaze never left her face. "You're simply repeating what you did for your father."

After finishing the glass of wine she no longer wanted, Emily excused herself on the pretext of being tired, his observation circling in her head.

Once back in her room, Emily found it difficult to settle.

Was Dalton right? Was she simply following old patterns even when given the opportunity to live life differently? Yet, with her money supply dipping into the danger zone, she'd needed a job and a place to stay. Had she really had a choice?

Emily wished Irene were here to advise her.

Striding to the dresser, Emily pulled out the box of letters, then rummaged through it until she found the letter she sought. She'd written it to Irene just after Vince had given her his ultimatum.

Dearest Irene,

If ever there was a time I need your wise counsel, it is now. Vince has made it clear he is moving to Baltimore to start his new job, with or without me.

He still wants to marry me, but says the job he accepted will not wait. He offered to find a place for my father, one that would offer him excellent care, and says that I may visit him as often as I desire.

I cannot seem to make Vincent understand my reluctance, even though I have explained that GraceTown is my father's home. It is where his friends are and where his physician is. Also, the hotel will need someone to oversee it until my father is better, and right now there are not the funds to hire or pay anyone.

You remember how good Papa was to me when my dear mama passed. He could have sent me to live with relatives, as many men do when they are widowed with young children, but he did not.

As I write this, I see that the heart of the matter is that I want to be the one to care for Papa until he is better, not put him away to be cared for by strangers.

There was more, pages and pages more. Once she'd gotten started writing, emotions had flowed out onto the paper like the water flowing in Cripple Creek after a heavy rain.

Writing the letter and picturing Irene, who'd known her better than anyone else, had helped. By the time she'd finished writing, it had become clear that Vince would be going to Baltimore, and she wouldn't be with him.

She'd given Vince his ring back and freed him of his obligation.

Deep down, she'd hoped that perhaps when her father was back on his feet, they...

Emily remembered clearly holding on to that scrap of hope during the following two years. Years in which her father had worked hard to walk again, to speak clearly. He'd nearly been able to function independently when he'd been felled by another stroke. Twenty-three months after his first stroke, he'd passed away.

After carefully placing the letter back where she had found it, Emily pushed to her feet and began to pace.

She had told herself that she'd accepted the position at Myra's home because it gave her everything she'd needed at the time—a roof over her head, an income and relative freedom.

Then why did Dalton's comment continue to niggle at her? Was she really squandering her do-over?

Taking out a sheet of paper, Emily began to write. But, for the first time, she couldn't picture Irene's face.

The pen faltered in her hand, and she set it down.

What was happening? Was this disconnect because of the elixir? Had the gift she'd been given affected her in more ways than simply the physical?

She was the same person, wasn't she?

Yes, she thought, *but no.*

Being young again, having people interact with her as a woman in her prime of life rather than a woman nearing the end of her life, provided different experiences.

She was not the same woman who'd swallowed the elixir. Yet, if Dalton was right, she was simply repeating the past in a different way.

Emily flung herself on the bed, buried her face in the pillows and let the tears fall.

Had drinking the potion been a mistake?

She'd yearned to carve out a life for herself without all the obligations and restrictions she'd faced during her life.

Now that she had the chance, she found herself scared, unsure and, most of all, incredibly lonely.

~

The next morning, Emily found Myra in the parlor at the game table, papers strewn before her.

"May I join you?" Emily asked, standing in the doorway. "Or are you working on something that needs total concentration and quiet?"

She figured asking this way allowed Myra to graciously say that she wanted to be left alone. Emily always kept in mind that this was Myra's home, not her own.

Looking up, Myra smiled and motioned Emily forward. "Please, join me. I'm working on several names that are particularly difficult. I hoped I might have better luck when I'm fresh."

"I'm happy to help." Emily took the seat opposite Myra. "If you'd like."

"I'd love your assistance and your company."

The housekeeper approached. "Mrs. Edwards, if there is anything you'd like to add to the grocery list, I'll be turning it in later today." Mrs. Fairfax glanced at Emily and smiled. "Good morning, Emily."

When the woman was out of earshot, Emily finally asked the question she kept meaning to ask. "Why the formality? I call you Myra, and you call me Emily. She's worked for you for years, but it's still so formal between you."

"It's her choice, not mine." Amusement flickered in Myra's eyes. "I would prefer different, but I respect her request."

Emily nodded.

"Tell me about the wedding." Myra set down the pencil in her hand.

Keeping it light, Emily gave Myra a rundown on the evening.

"It sounds perfectly lovely," Myra said when she'd finished. "I'm extremely happy to hear that the food from the Manse was a hit."

"Jaclyn appears to have found her niche." Emily's smile faded. "I wish I could find my calling."

The questioning look in Myra's eyes had Emily admitting, "I woke up this morning to two rejection letters in my inbox."

"What kind of rejection letters?"

"From two out of the three private schools I applied to." Emily expelled a breath. "I'm not exactly sure what to do next. I only know I don't want to go back to playing with a symphony."

Myra took a sip from her glass of what looked like raspberry lemonade. "Why not?"

A straightforward question demanded a straightforward answer.

"Playing with a symphony takes over your life. Or, at least, it can." Emily met Myra's questioning gaze. "As much as I love music, and I adore playing the violin, I want more out of my life."

"What are you considering?"

"For me, teaching in a school system would be ideal. It would allow me to incorporate my love of teaching with my love of music. Unfortunately, there's only one school left that's a possibility."

"Which one is that?" Myra asked.

"Crestwood Academy."

"It's an excellent school. Walt went there, as did Kenneth."

"From what I've read, it has a robust music program. If the position there doesn't come through, I'm thinking I could teach one-on-one. Either online or in person or both. I'm also looking at what opportunities are available as a music therapist at a hospital or retirement community."

"All good options. Before you put too much pressure on yourself to get it right the first time, just remember that whatever position you take doesn't have to be a forever kind of thing. You give it a try, if it doesn't work, you try something else." Myra offered a supportive smile. "I believe you'll do well no matter what path you choose. You're a well-educated woman with amazing people skills and incredible musical talent. That's a recipe for success in any book."

Emily's heart swelled. "Thank you."

"If you need a regular paycheck until you find something that's more what you're looking for, I'd be happy to speak with Ken and see if he has any openings at the Oasis."

"I appreciate the offer, I really do." There had been a time not that long ago that Emily would have jumped at the chance to work at the Oasis, side by side with Chloe. "But I fear I won't get anywhere if I hold on to the side of the swimming pool."

Puzzlement filled the older woman's eyes. "What swimming pool?"

"It's a metaphor for not going all in. For not taking risks." Emily hesitated. "It happens when a person is unwilling to let go of the safe and the familiar. Being adventurous is difficult for me since I'm also pragmatic."

Myra quirked an eyebrow. "Some might disagree with you on that point. After all, is it pragmatic to quit a steady job and move to a city with no job and no connections?"

Emily gnawed her lip. It was still easy to forget that people knew her only as Emily, not Til. "It was, when I had savings to fall back on, at least for a while."

Myra nodded in agreement. "While being pragmatic is good, I applaud your efforts to go after what you want. When I look back on my life, all of my regrets are from when I played it safe."

The next morning, Emily agreed to accompany Myra to Maplewood Park, where they would meet with the women on the renovation committee.

"Beverly is bringing homemade cinnamon buns," Myra told her on the drive over. "I offered to bring something, but she made it clear they had today's treats covered. Geraldine told me to enjoy and warned that my turn is coming." Her lips turned up in a little smile. "Geraldine is a real character. You can't help but love her."

Emily only nodded and wheeled the vehicle into the park's small parking lot. She didn't want to say too much and give away just how well she knew these women.

They found Beverly, Geraldine, Lisa and Jenna in the process of setting out the treats on a rickety old picnic table.

Someone had had the forethought to bring a red checkered oilcloth to spread across the table.

When she and Myra strolled up, the women turned.

"I hoped you'd bring Emily." Beverly offered her a welcoming smile. "This way, we have two young ones to keep us oldsters on track."

Jenna rolled her eyes. "I'm glad Emily is here, too, but we all know you 'oldsters' can run rings around us youngsters."

Geraldine chuckled. "No argument here."

The comment made everyone laugh.

"I took the liberty of outlining nine steps necessary to move forward with this project." Myra pulled six sheets of paper from her handbag. "I made copies for everyone."

Jenna took one and quickly scanned the document. "In order to determine how the improvements align with community needs and interests, we probably should contact the city planning commission for that information."

"Good idea." Myra smiled. "Will you handle that?"

"Happy to," Jenna agreed.

Emily hid a smile. It was the old *you bring it up, you get assigned the task*.

"Today, we should be able to complete number two on the list." Geraldine pointed to the paper she'd placed to the right of the plate holding her cinnamon bun. "We can easily identify the areas that need improvement."

"Which is pretty much everything," Beverly quipped, earning a smile from everyone.

Emily tapped her lips and considered. "We might want to speak with someone at Leaves of Green and get the names of landscape architects they recommend. Get the ball rolling in that area."

"Fabulous suggestion." Myra gave an approving nod.

"Is that something you could handle, Emily?" Lisa asked. "If not, I—"

"I'd be happy to take that on." Emily told herself that even if she did get one of the jobs she'd applied for, this task would involve making only one quick phone call.

"I can research the necessary approvals and permits." Lisa smiled. "As a librarian, this kind of research is right up my alley."

"Thank you, Lisa." Myra offered the woman a warm smile. "Your expertise is very much appreciated."

Geraldine had brought her tool kit, so after they finished eating, she worked her magic on several unsteady benches that would likely need to be replaced. "I could fix the merry-go-round, but it's the type no longer used because of safety concerns."

"Best to leave it as it is," Jenna announced, and the others nodded in agreement.

Once a list had been made of areas needing improvement, they set another date and time to meet and headed home.

When Emily and Myra arrived home, they found Ken pacing the porch.

"Where have you been?" he demanded, hurrying down the steps to meet them as they stepped from the Lincoln. His gaze narrowed on his mother. "Why haven't you answered your phone?"

"Don't talk to me in that tone, Kenneth." Myra's eyes turned cool. "I'm sorry I worried you. I left my phone at home. I was at a meeting of the Maplewood Park renovation committee. And, before you ask, the AED is in my bag."

Wanting to give the two some privacy, Emily turned, intending to slip into the house.

Myra stopped her with a hand on her arm. "Before you go, thank you for today."

Conscious of Ken's eyes on her, Emily only shrugged. "I didn't do anything. Except drive you over."

"You did far more, and you know it." Myra squeezed her arm. "Thank you."

"You're welcome." Emily turned back to Ken. "Nice to see you again."

Once inside, Emily learned from Mrs. Fairfax that Ken was there to take his mother to an appointment with her cardiologist.

Emily pulled her brows together. "It surprises me that Myra forgot about the appointment."

Mrs. Fairfax, a thin woman with steel-rimmed glasses that matched her hair, waved an airy hand. "Mr. Edwards said something about the visit being the result of a last-minute cancellation. He probably assumed she'd be here. After all, until you came along, she never went anywhere." The housekeeper fixed her gaze on Emily. "You've changed her life."

"I haven't—" Emily began.

"I heard her telling Mr. Edwards yesterday that she's seriously considering having the surgery." Mrs. Fairfax's expression remained serious. "That's likely what this appointment is about. You may soon find yourself out of a job."

Emily smiled. "I can't think of a better reason to get the boot."

CHAPTER NINETEEN

Mrs. Fairfax's warning rang in her ears as Emily hopped onto her bike and headed downtown. She wasn't nearly as cavalier about losing her position as she'd made it sound.

She reassured herself that all she needed was enough money coming in to cover basic living expenses. If she had to have five roommates and share a bathroom to make that happen, that's what she'd do.

Minutes later, she stepped into the warm friendliness of Cuppa Joe. When she found herself wishing she was meeting a friend, she shoved the self-pitying thought aside.

After getting her latte, she took it to a nearby table. Once seated, she pulled out a small notebook and a pencil.

While she knew any note-taking could easily be done on her phone, she believed that her particular brain was more creative when she wrote things out.

Music

Tapping her pencil against the table, she took a long sip of her latte and wrote her notes.

Crestwood Academy—follow up on application

Research best practices for teaching music classes online and in person

Contact GraceTown General Hospital re music therapy pos—

"You're looking way too serious for a Monday morning."

She looked up into the teasing eyes of Dalton.

"Simply doing a little life planning." She gestured to the empty chair at the table. "Please, join me."

"Don't mind if I do." He dropped down and set his ceramic coffee cup on the table. "Tell me about this life planning."

Emily closed the small notebook. "Nothing has been decided yet."

"I hope you know that your job with Gran is secure."

"It's only temporary." The contract she'd signed had been for thirty days. That meant a mere nine days from now she would be out of a job…and a place to live. "Once your grandmother has the procedure, she'll have no need for me."

Surprise skittered across Dalton's face. "Has she decided to do it?"

"I don't know for sure, but Mrs. Fairfax seems to think so. She and your father are meeting with the cardiologist this morning."

Dalton smiled broadly. "That is good news."

"It is."

"What's on tap for you today?"

"Right now?" She lifted her cup. "Finish my latte."

"Would you like to cross something off your wish list?"

She pulled her brows together. "Wish list?"

"You told me you once dreamed of getting in a convertible and driving with no real destination in mind." He cocked his head. "Is that still something you'd like to do?"

"Yes." She smiled. "But I don't have a convertible."

"I do." Dalton downed the rest of his coffee. "And I happen to have the rest of the day free. Interested?"

Emily left her bike locked up in front of Cuppa Joe and strolled with Dalton to his car.

Once he was behind the wheel, he slanted a questioning glance in her direction. "Where to?"

"No particular destination."

"Works for me." He put the car in reverse at the same time his phone rang. "Hold on a second."

He answered without putting the phone on speaker, so Emily could hear only his part of the conversation. "Hey, Jaclyn, what's up?"

His brows pulled together, and he frowned. "Then don't meet her. Just because she's in the area doesn't mean you have to rearrange your life to suit hers. No, she hasn't contacted me."

When he hung up, he turned to Emily. "Apparently, my mother is going to be in Baltimore tomorrow. She texted Jaclyn about getting together."

"Your parents are divorced." Emily had known his parents weren't together, and hadn't been for years, but that was the extent of her knowledge.

"Since I was sixteen. Mom wanted out. Even before the divorce was final, she and her new friend moved to Florida." Dalton offered a sardonic smile. "As he wasn't keen on starting off their life together with two teenage kids, my mom gave my dad full custody in exchange for a generous financial settlement."

"Did you see her much as a teen?"

A muscle in his jaw jumped. "Dad attempted to help us stay in touch, but she always had an excuse why visiting her wouldn't work."

"Do you have contact with her now?"

Dalton's gaze turned distant. "I don't, but she and Jaclyn text occasionally."

"I'm sorry. I can't imagine how hard that must be on you and your sister."

"Not as difficult as you might think." His eyes grew dark with memories. "During those last couple of years before they split, our home was a battleground. The only thing worse than hearing them argue was the tense silence that followed a big fight."

Emily wondered what it would be like to live with a spouse you argued with all of the time, or live in an environment where the air in the house was thick with unexpressed emotions.

Over the years, more than one woman had told her she was lucky to be single. That you could be lonely even while married and that at least she didn't have to ask a husband's permission to do what she wanted.

Dalton backed the car out of the driveway. "Which way?"

Emily blinked, then quickly rallied and gestured the toward the closest way out of town.

A light breeze ruffled her hair. Leaning back against the seat, she smiled. "This is how I envisioned a road trip."

"Except you dreamed of doing this alone," Dalton reminded her, a slight smile tugging at the corners of his lips. "Instead, you're stuck with me."

"Being with you isn't so bad."

They drove for several miles before they reached a fork in the road. "Stay straight or curve right?"

"Doesn't matter."

"Your choice."

Emily wanted to tell him that she had too many choices right now in her life, that he could decide. Until she recalled their talk about committing to a specific direction.

He was right. Her fantasy trip. Her choice. "Curve right."

When he wheeled the vehicle in that direction, Emily smiled. "I know what you're doing."

"Taking a drive?"

"You're trying to show me that I need a plan and a direction."

His lips quirked upward. "Is that what I'm doing?"

Emily saw the next turnoff up ahead, and before he had a chance to ask, she gestured. "Stay straight."

"Roger that."

"I know I need to find some direction in life." She blew out a breath. "While these past few weeks have been fun and full of new experiences, I need a plan going forward." She gave a little laugh. "I've never been great at making decisions. I was always more of a do-what-needs-to-be-done kind of person."

"Give yourself more credit. You were making a plan when I came upon you in the coffee shop. You have an idea where you want to be, what you want your life to look like."

"I don't. Not really." The realization had her frowning.

"I believe you do." Dalton slanted another glance in her direction as they approached another fork in the road. "You just need to get out of your head and follow your gut."

After picking up her bike at Cuppa Joe, Emily headed home. She didn't bother to text Chloe or Jaclyn or Mackenna. It was a work night. She already knew they wouldn't be interested in going out.

No matter, Emily thought as she climbed the porch steps. She'd always been good at entertaining herself.

Passing the parlor on the way to her room, she spotted Myra sitting in a tall wingback chair. A book lay open on her lap, but her head was tilted back, and her eyes were closed.

Alarm skittered through Emily with the force of a flash fire.

She hurried across the room. "Myra, are you okay?"

The woman's eyes instantly opened, and Myra blinked several times, then gave an embarrassed laugh. "Oh, sorry. I must have fallen asleep."

Expelling the breath that she hadn't realized she'd been holding, Emily sank onto the sofa. "You scared the bejesus out of me."

"I'm sorry I frightened you." Myra offered an apologetic smile. "While the visit with Dr. Hobart went well, I found it somewhat stressful."

"Stressful in what way?" Emily asked, then added, "If you don't mind my asking, that is."

"I don't mind. Dr. Hobart explained the risks and benefits of the procedure." Myra waved a dismissive hand. "While it was nothing I hadn't heard before, having the procedure scheduled for Friday—"

"This Friday?" Emily's voice rose, then cracked.

"Exactly my response." Myra chuckled, then quickly sobered. "He's worried about me having some...event...and doesn't want to wait any longer now that I've made up my mind to have it done. According to him, I'm extremely fortunate nothing has occurred yet." Leaning over, Myra took Emily's hand for a second and gave it a quick squeeze. "My decision to have this done is because of you."

Emily held up her hands, palms out. "Hey, I don't know anything about what they want to do—"

"No, but you believe I still have a lot to live for, and now I believe that myself." Myra sat back in her chair. "I'd convinced myself that when Walt died that my life was over. Thanks to you, I no longer believe that's true."

Emily knew that Myra was the one who'd taken the opportunities Emily had put in front of her and run with them. "How long will you be in the hospital?"

"Not long, since we're going with a newer type of implantable defibrillator, a subcutaneous one. My understanding is that while the leads and the generator will be under the skin, unlike the conventional type, the leads for this one won't be in the heart itself."

"That's nice, I guess."

"I think so." Myra smiled. "Dr. Hobart will have his partner— an electrophysiologist, a cardiologist who specializes in arrhythmia—do the procedure."

"You'll be in the hospital for a few days, maybe a week?" Emily was already planning what activities she could bring to the hospital when she visited, but Myra laughed.

"Dr. Hobart said I might go home the same day, or at most, spend the night in the hospital."

"Really?"

"Surprised me, too." Myra closed the book on her lap. "Apparently, most patients return to light to moderate activities within a few days."

"I'm guessing no contact sports."

"He actually told me that." Myra laughed and shook her head. "I'm apprehensive, yes, but now that I've decided, I'm eager to get it over with."

"If there's anything I can do—"

"You've already done it." Myra met her gaze. "I've loved having you here with me."

It was almost, but not quite, a good-bye.

Emily knew if she asked, Myra would let her stay past her contract date, but she also knew she couldn't stay forever.

When she reached her bedroom, Emily flopped back on the bed. Had it really been only a month since she had sat with her friends, playing cards and talking about do-overs?

Right now, it felt like forever.

She'd had such high hopes when she'd drunk the liquid.

What she hadn't realized was how much she'd miss her friends and her house and her garden. And she still didn't understand why people like Irene died so young and other people lived into their nineties.

She sure hadn't expected to feel so lost about how to forge ahead in this new life.

Maybe she should have walked away from Serena Nordine and never drunk the youth elixir. Maybe it would have been better if she'd left well enough alone.

∾

Myra came home the same day she had the surgery, and her family was all there waiting for her. After giving Myra a hug, Emily left her with her son and grandchildren and took off on her bike.

She couldn't recall ever feeling this low, this alone in the world. Hoping exercise would shake off the melancholy, Emily rode her bike, ending up at Maplewood Park.

Despite its state of disrepair, the grounds of the park still felt like home. Attaching her bike to the lone bike rack, Emily headed to the bench by the hollyhocks.

When it came into view, she came to an abrupt stop.

There, sitting on the bench as she'd been a month earlier, was Serena Nordine.

Today, the red highlights were gone, and she'd pulled her dark hair into a high pony. The shorts and top had been replaced by a white summer dress. But the intensity in her vivid blue eyes was the same as she settled her gaze on Emily.

"Serena. I didn't expect to see you here." Emily moved forward as everything in her quivered. She hadn't expected to see Serena ever again.

"It's good to see you, Emily." Serena patted the bench beside her. "Sit."

Once Emily sat, Serena shifted her body to face her. Those blue eyes—violet, really—searched hers. "How have you been?"

The concern in Serena's eyes and the warmth in her tone had Emily relaxing.

"I'm...adjusting." Emily spoke cautiously, not sure what the endgame was here. "It's been difficult."

"You're not happy."

"Things haven't gone quite the way I thought they would." Emily gave a little laugh. "But I'm persevering. I'll make the best of it."

"You don't need to."

Emily stilled. "I don't understand."

"I'm here to offer you the chance to undo it all, to go back to being Til."

"What?" Emily blinked, and her heart shifted into overdrive. "How would that work?"

"Well, it starts the same." As she had before, Serena pulled out a small, beautiful vial. This time, however, she didn't immediately pass it to Emily. "Unlike before, you won't take anything with you, not the memories of your new experiences, not your musical talent." Serena's tone was matter-of-fact. "Myra will not have had her surgery or become friends with Til's friends. It will be as if the past four weeks never happened."

"You can do that?"

Serena nodded.

Emily's mind whirled. Was this not the very question she had been pondering? Had becoming Emily been a mistake? Would it have been better to stay Matilda and leave her life unchanged? Sure, she'd have her ninety-two-year-old body back and fewer years ahead, but she'd also have her friends.

"I can give you twenty-four hours to say your final good-byes." Serena's gaze searched hers. She set the bottle on the bench between them. "The choice is yours. But you must be certain, because this change cannot be undone."

CHAPTER TWENTY

The next day dawned bright and clear on Matilda Beemis's celebration-of-life service.

Beverly and Geraldine had offered to host the event at their home, but those plans changed when it appeared that a large number of people in the community planned to show up.

Word was, the *Gazette* was even sending a reporter and news crew to cover the event. For that reason, the decision had been made to hold the memorial at the local civic center.

Emily wasn't sure how one dressed for their own memorial service, but she brought out the little black dress she'd worn to Rosemary's reception.

"I wish you would ride with us." Myra stood as Emily came down the hall.

The entire family was attending the service and were now gathered in the parlor.

Dalton stood by the mantel. "There is plenty of room."

"It's a beautiful day, and I feel like walking." Emily gestured to her flats. "These are extremely comfortable."

"You look quite lovely, my dear." Myra offered Emily a reassuring smile.

"I understand you'll be playing your violin at the service." Ken took a sip of coffee.

"Yes." Emily swallowed, her throat having suddenly gone bone-dry. "Her-her friends asked if I'd play 'Amazing Grace.' Apparently, it was a favorite of hers."

Myra expelled a breath. "That tune always brings a tear to my eye."

It always brought a tear to Emily's eyes as well. Which was exactly why she really hadn't wanted to play it. But she could tell it meant a lot to the women who meant so much to her. Which was why she'd agreed.

"It does tug at the heartstrings," Emily said when she noticed Myra gazing expectantly at her. Picking up the case she'd set at her feet, Emily slung it over her shoulder. "I better go. I promised to meet Lola before the ceremony begins."

When she'd been asked to play, Emily had mentioned Lola. The women had enthusiastically approved of her suggestion that she and Lola perform together.

"I can come with you." Dalton set his cup on the mantel. "Keep you company."

"Thank you, but I need this time to mentally prepare." Emily shrugged. "Like for your grandmother, 'Amazing Grace' is one of those tunes that brings all sorts of memories flooding back."

Ken's expression remained solemn. "It seems like it is played at every memorial service or funeral I've attended."

"It was played at my mother's and at my father's." A lump formed in Emily's throat. She cleared it before continuing. "I need to focus on this being about Matilda."

"If you change your mind on the walk over," Dalton held up his phone, "I'm driving separately, so just call."

"I will." Emily smiled at him, grateful he understood. Grateful they all understood.

～

The staff of the civic center was bringing in extra chairs when Emily arrived. Though the service wasn't set to begin for thirty minutes, the auditorium was already three-quarters full.

The front of the auditorium was filled with flowers, not just the brightly colored ones Til had adored, but everything from peace lilies—a standard at any funeral/memorial service—to roses in every color.

The hollyhock display had Emily blinking back tears when she turned to greet Lola.

"OMG, when you said this was a celebration-of-life service for an old woman, I thought twenty or thirty people would show." Lola's eyes were wide as she glanced around the large room. "There must be a hundred people here already, with more streaming in every minute."

Emily had mentioned that Til was ninety-two and active in the community. While she might have expected more than twenty or thirty people coming to pay their respects, the number of people who were showing up surprised even her.

"Is there anything I can do to help you set up?" Emily asked.

Lola had already been here when Emily had arrived, and from the looks of it, all the equipment was ready to go—including a video camera.

"Are you going to record this?" Emily asked. That hadn't been part of the discussion.

A watchful look filled Lola's eyes. "I thought I would, unless you have objections."

"What are you going to do with the footage?"

"I'm not sure yet." Lola's expression grew thoughtful. "I thought I would put the 'Amazing Grace' rendition up on TikTok, along with a kind of memorial message."

"Why?"

"Because it's 'Amazing Grace.'" Lola shot her a quick smile. "And because we're going to be amazing."

Emily tapped two fingers against her lips. She was still trying to figure out this social media stuff. "I don't know..."

"How about we record it, and then we can talk about it and decide?"

"That will work."

~

By the time the service started, the room was bursting at the seams. From where she was seated off to the side, Emily recognized so many in attendance.

Even former inmates whom she'd tutored at the detention facility, some from way back when she'd first begun her literacy efforts, had come. Many had brought their families with them.

Her heart swelled as she recalled Jose, who now ran a successful plumbing business in GraceTown, and how he had flawlessly read an entire page in English. Or Maury, from youth detention, who'd been passed on from one grade to the next in school without learning to read. His dyslexia had meant that an alternate method of learning had had to be employed.

So many students who'd become productive members of society and valued friends through the years were here.

Sally, whom she had been proud to call a neighbor and whom she'd seen on her way to the park that last fateful day, was here, along with her family.

Lisa had volunteered to be the emcee for the service. As a librarian, Lisa was comfortable in front of a crowd. It must be a good day for her MS, because she walked with her son's assistance to the podium, her wheelchair nowhere in sight.

"Thank you all for coming here today to honor the life of your friend and mine, Matilda Beemis." Lisa let her gaze sweep the crowd, and her lips curved up ever so slightly. "I think we can all agree that Til was a force of nature and a woman we will never forget."

Beverly stepped to the podium then.

Emily hid her surprise. Beverly must have insisted on being a part of the service, because Emily knew the other friends would not have forced her, knowing how nervous she got when speaking to a group.

"We spent a lot of time on this obituary, so for those of you who missed it, I'm going to read it now." Beverly appeared to relax as laughter rippled through the crowd. "This is only a snapshot and certainly not the whole of a life well lived."

Beverly paused, as if to make sure she had everyone's attention, then continued. "Matilda Jean Beemis was born..."

Emily listened, amazed at the details that her friends had included and how they added to her life story without being boring.

"Wow," Lola whispered. "I'm impressed."

Emily only nodded, noticing Beverly appeared to be nearing the end of her reading.

"When someone reaches the ripe old age of ninety-two, you know their days could be numbered." Beverly paused, clearly overcome with emotion. "But you're never prepared to lose a friend. Especially not one like her."

Lisa, who'd taken a seat near the podium, rose and moved to Beverly, sliding an arm around her friend's shoulders.

"We miss Til, but we know she's not truly gone."

Was it only Emily's imagination, or did Lisa glance in her direction?

"She is still with us, and her works and her caring will live on in our memories," Lisa said solemnly.

Beverly leaned toward the microphone, having regained her composure. "At this point in the service, I would welcome those of you who knew Til, whose lives were touched by her, to come forward and share your experience."

A dark-haired man who looked vaguely familiar to Emily was the first one to reach the podium.

"Miss Beemis was my tutor when I first came to this country. I was eight and having a difficult time in school because of not knowing the language." The man spoke quickly, his words tumbling out. "She helped me learn to read, and then, while she worked with my older sister, her granddaughter, Chloe, and I would sit and talk."

The man gave a little laugh. "I didn't realize until much later that that was part of my lesson, working on my conversational skills. Our parents only spoke Spanish at home, and my sister and I didn't say much at school because we were embarrassed. But it was fun talking to Chloe. I hope both of them knew just what a difference they made in our lives."

He might have been the first, but he wasn't the last one to step to the podium.

Emily was amazed and touched. She'd never been formally honored for her accomplishments and hadn't seen her efforts as anything special. Not when she looked around and saw others who seemed to be doing so much more.

But now, listening to person after person talk about how her help, however little it might have been, had changed their lives made her realize that she'd put her mark on this earth, through all the people she'd helped.

"Thank you all for sharing how Til impacted your life." Beverly smiled. "I like to think she is with us now, seeing all her friends, listening to the stories, remembering right along with you and me and smiling that warm, wonderful smile of hers."

"One of the things that Til always said warmed her heart at services like these were the songs," Lisa said. "Her favorite was 'Amazing Grace.'" Lisa glanced over to where Lola and Emily waited for the signal to begin. "Today, we have Emily Curtis and Lola Whitehead, two talented musicians, to play that song for us."

It took all the strength Emily possessed to continue to play when Lola began to sing. Between the heartfelt emotion coming from the violin and the words that had always touched her heart, she wasn't sure she could keep her emotions in check.

She told herself she owed it to all these people who had come here today to pay their respects to keep it together.

When the song concluded, dead silence filled the auditorium.

Then a couple of people began to clap, then others joined in. Emily knew clapping at a memorial service wasn't customary, but nothing about Til's death was customary. And it was apparent the song had moved many in the audience.

Emily bowed her head in acknowledgment, and Lola did the same.

When the applause faded, Lisa stepped back to the podium.

"I don't know about you, but this service honoring our dear friend has inspired me. When I go home tonight, I'm going to figure out how I can do more to make this world, and especially GraceTown, a better place."

Another round of applause greeted the sentiment.

"For now, enjoy cupcakes—made by my daughter-in-law, so I can vouch for their deliciousness—and punch on the back terrace. We invite you to gather and share your Til stories with each other." Lisa held up a hand as people began to rise. "I would also like to announce that the efforts to restore Maplewood Park as a way of honoring her are moving forward. Look for a future article in the *Gazette* on how you can help and also on efforts to give this park that Til loved a new name—Beemis Park. Thank you all for coming."

Emily and Lola began to pack up their equipment as everyone filed out of the room and headed in the direction of the terrace.

"You sang beautifully, Lola. Thank you."

"I always want to do my best, but I admit after listening to all the stories, I really wanted to do it as a tribute to her." Lola shook her head. "I wish I'd had a chance to meet her. She sounds like an amazing woman. Andrew certainly thought a lot of her."

Emily had nearly forgotten that Lola and Andrew, the young

man who'd always helped her at Timeless Treasures, were dating. "You two are still seeing each other?"

"For now. He's a nice guy. I'm just not ready to get involved on a more serious level." Lola slanted a sideways glance at Emily as she put away the amplifier. "What about you?"

"I don't have the time to get serious with anyone."

Lola gestured with his head. "Not even with him?"

Emily looked up, and there was Dalton, striding straight toward her.

CHAPTER TWENTY-ONE

Emily might have accepted Dalton's offer to grab a drink if Jenna hadn't already asked her over to her and Daniel's house, where close friends of Til were gathering.

Dalton then said he'd give her a ride to the Graces' house. Though the home was within easy walking distance, Emily felt exhausted. She wasn't sure going to this gathering was a good idea with her emotions so close to the surface, but she felt as if it was where she was meant to be.

"That's an honor that they invited you to join them." Dalton opened the car door, then shut it once she'd slid inside.

Emily shrugged. "I was surprised, but flattered."

"If you need a ride home once you're done, give me a call."

"If I need a ride, I bet someone will give me a lift. Or I can call an Uber."

"Please call me if you need a ride."

"I will." Promising seemed like such a small thing. The last thing she wanted was for him to worry about her. "Could you do me a favor?"

"Anything."

"Don't be so quick to agree." Emily's tone turned teasing. "You don't know what I'm going to ask."

"Whatever you ask, I'll say yes."

Emily laughed. They both know that wasn't true. She gestured with one hand toward the back of the car where she'd stowed her violin case. "Would you mind taking my instrument case to your grandmother's house? You can just set it outside the door to my bedroom."

"I can do that." He inclined his head. "How's the apartment hunting coming?"

Emily just shrugged again.

"You know there's no rush." When he stopped at a light, Dalton shifted in his seat to face her. "Gran loves having you around."

The light changed, and Dalton's eyes returned to the road.

"I've enjoyed getting to know your grandmother," Emily said, with emotion. "And you."

She expelled a sigh.

Dalton pulled the BMW to a stop in front of the Grace home. His expression turned serious. "You make it sound so final. You're not getting rid of either of us that easily."

Hearing the concern in his voice, seeing the worry in his eyes, Emily reached over and gave his hand a squeeze. "I need to do what feels right to me."

His blue eyes met hers. "Only if you're sure."

There was something about the concern, the protectiveness, that touched a raw spot deep inside.

Impulsively, she leaned forward and kissed him gently on the mouth. "Thank you."

Though his eyes remained serious, he smiled. "What was that for?"

"Let's just say, in honor of Matilda Beemis, I'm seizing the moment." Emily opened the door of the convertible and stepped out. When she shut it, she leaned over the side. "You're a good guy, Dalton Edwards. You are definitely not someone easily forgotten."

~

Emily knew that she shouldn't have been surprised that the gathering at Jenna's home was a lighthearted, festive one, instead of a somber affair. These were her friends, and they were well aware that she wouldn't want them to be draped in black and sorrow.

Her heart gave a little leap when she spotted Chloe across the room speaking with Geraldine.

While she watched the two, Hannah stepped to her side, drawing her attention away.

"It was a lovely celebration. You and Lola's rendition of 'Amazing Grace' brought tears to my eyes."

"To mine as well." Just thinking of seeing all her friends gathered together honoring *her* had been humbling.

Hannah handed her a glass of punch. "Tropical passion. I seem to recall it's one of your favorites."

It had been Til's favorite, but as far as Emily knew, she'd never expressed a liking for it. Unless, maybe, she had. "Thank you, and yes, the celebration of life you and the others organized, well, I think your friend would have approved."

Hannah's smile lit her entire face. "I'll let everyone know. It will mean a lot to them."

Chloe came in and made a beeline straight for Emily. She wrapped her arms around her in a fierce hug. "Thank you so much."

"What did I do?" Emily asked when she stepped back.

"'Amazing Grace' performed by you and Lola was the perfect way to cap off Til's perfectly amazing life." For a second, Chloe's eyes filled with tears, but she blinked them away. "I think our goal should be to live a life where, in the end, people say the same wonderful things about us."

"While I agree that it's nice to be remembered fondly, the real prize is having the chance to meet all the people Matilda knew, to share in their triumphs and their trials, too." Emily spoke softly, as if to herself. "It's easy to think of opportunity as only applying to the big stuff—the opportunity to travel, to get the dream job, to meet the perfect partner. But Matilda's life gave her the opportunity to fill the world with goodness and love. We should all be so lucky."

Why was it that the decision she needed to make suddenly seemed so very easy?

~

One month later, Chloe officially took possession of Til's bungalow. When she moved in, Emily moved in with her.

"You really should have the primary bedroom," Emily told Chloe. "It's bigger."

"Not by much. Besides, this was always my bedroom. I like it better." Chloe glanced at the sewing machine by the window. "Do you know how to sew?"

"I do," Emily admitted, glancing at the vintage Singer purchased decades ago.

"Even on a machine as ancient as this one?"

"It's still got a lot of good years left in her."

"Speaking of ancient, Jaclyn mentioned that you're playing cards with the old ladies this week."

"Lisa had plans so I was invited to sub. It's at Myra's house this week." Emily's lips curved. She couldn't wait to play cards with her friends again. "And for your information those ladies are awesome, and they're my friends. It makes no difference how old they are."

"I suppose," Chloe conceded then changed the subject. "Are you excited about your new position?"

Emily hung up the dresses in her hand, then dropped to sit on the daybed. "I really am. Myra really came through for me. Because of her call to the headmistress at Crestwood, I have a teaching position in their music department."

"She's amazing."

Emily glanced at Chloe's closet. "Since you're nearly done in here, I'm going to work on mine."

She turned toward the door, then whirled back. "I keep forgetting to ask—what do you want me to do with Til's clothes?"

"I guess I haven't thought that far." Concern furrowed Chloe's brow. "I really don't want to trash them."

"Have you thought about donating? They're in good shape. I'm betting someone will want them."

"I like that idea." Chloe's eyes lit up. "Let's do that. I'll help you box them up once I'm finished in here."

"No rush." Emily thought the task would be easy and quick, but discovered clothing held memories. As she carefully folded and boxed dresses, slacks and tops, thoughts of events she'd attended and people she'd been with when wearing the clothing kept surfacing.

Those memories were ones she would hold tight, as well as so many more. She thought of that warm summer day when she'd sat beside Serena Nordine on that park bench and been offered a do-over. She'd seen the elixir as a reward for a lifetime of sacrifice.

It was now clear to her that Til's life hadn't been about sacrifice, but about caring. She'd cared for her father and for Chloe and all those needing a hand up, because that's who she was. She gave, not because she expected anything back, but simply because, deep down, she was a giver, and giving brought her joy.

In turn, she had been blessed with a life that had been incredibly rich and full.

Her new life, her second chance, well, these past months had been a time of discovery.

Emily now realized that life wasn't all about her, it was about what she could do to help other people make their lives better. By doing that, it made her own better.

She was so grateful to Serena for this opportunity. It had allowed her to help Myra and Chloe and to discover so many unexpected, wonderful things.

Her lips curved as she thought of Dalton and their relationship that was still shiny and new.

A knock at the front door had her calling out to Chloe. "I'll get it."

Emily smiled at the sight of Myra, Dalton and Jaclyn standing on the porch.

"I hope we're not intruding—" Myra began.

"Absolutely not." Emily stepped back and motioned them inside. "Please, come in. This is a nice surprise."

"We brought you a housewarming present." Jaclyn held out a bamboo plant sporting a big red bow.

"Jenna and Rosemary said bamboo symbolizes strength and resilience, which is something you and Chloe have in spades," Myra informed them with a smile.

"Who was at—?" Chloe's face lit up when she saw them.

"They brought us a housewarming gift." Emily handed the plant to her. "Isn't it lovely?"

"I love it. And I know just where I'm going to put it." Instead of hurrying off, Chloe paused. "Can I get you all something to drink? Emily made lemonade this morning. Real lemonade, from the fruit of the lemon tree in Jenna's backyard."

Myra glanced at her grandchildren. "I have time if you do."

Jaclyn smiled at Emily and Chloe. "I've got time."

"I see no reason to rush off," Dalton told his grandmother, before shifting his focus to Emily. His gaze seemed to linger on her mouth.

Jaclyn moved to Chloe's side. "I'll help you."

"How are you liking your new space?" Myra asked Emily, taking a seat on the sofa.

"I like it very much."

"She has to say that," Chloe called over her shoulder, "because I'm standing right here."

Emily laughed, then turned to Myra. "While I already know I'm going to love it here, I miss you already."

"The house seems empty without you. No dominoes, checkers or late-night chats. And no anagram help." Myra offered a melodramatic sigh before her expression brightened. "I forgot to tell you. I finally unscrambled that name you gave me."

Emily pulled her brows together. "Which one?"

"Serena Nordine."

"What other name does it make?" Emily asked.

"Irene Anderson."

That night, from the comfort of her new—old—bedroom, Emily sat at the tiny desk by the window and penned her last letter to Irene.

Dearest Irene, or should I say Serena?

You truly have been the most wonderful of friends. When you promised that you would always be with me, you meant it.

Writing to you all these years has been such a comfort. When I saw you in the park, I knew there was something special about you. I trusted you even though I believed you a stranger.

I only wish you could have told me that you were my bosom friend who I've missed all these years. I would have given you the biggest hug.

The words "for such a time as this" circle in my head. You came back into my life, bearing your special gift, at precisely the right time. I doubt I'd have been in the position to help Myra and Chloe otherwise. I believe they will both continue to do wonderful things.

Remember our pinkie promises? Well, I pinkie promise that I will consider the world my oyster and aim high.

Emily paused, considering what name to sign.

Her lips curved. It was full steam ahead with a focus on the future.

She brought her pencil back to the paper and wrote:

Much love always,

Emily

Now that you've finished The Youth Elixir, I hope you're ready to see your favorite characters again when you return to this town known for the unexplainable.

Although each book in the series can be read separately, I love bringing back characters from earlier books. This means you'll see many of these fantastic women (and men!) in the next book in the series, THE NOTE KEEPER.

Taylor Higgs' father once promised her that, like a compass, he may not always show her the way, but he'd be there to point her in the right direction. During her childhood, he frequently wrote her notes of encouragement, filled with his own brand of wisdom. After his unexpected death, Taylor feels lost and adrift... until notes begin showing up in the pocket of his favorite coat. Notes directed to her, with messages designed to help her navigate the most challenging time in her life...

Trust me, you don't want to miss this captivating tale of heartfelt love and unwavering devotion. Grab your copy today.

SNEAK PEEK OF THE NOTEKEEPER

Chapter One

Taylor Higgs paused outside the door to Elite Sleuth Solutions. Seeing the name Robert Higgs, Private Investigator, etched in the glass, had her heart lurching. Her father had founded the business seven years earlier when he'd retired from the GraceTown police force.

He'd been so proud of running his own company and excited to be his own boss. While he had always enjoyed being a detective for GraceTown PD, he liked the autonomy of setting his own hours and taking on cases that mattered to him.

She knew he'd looked forward to many more years doing what he loved, but that hadn't been in the cards.

Taking a deep breath, Taylor pushed open the door, setting the bells to jingling. It was wild to think that her father had been in this office for over two years, yet this was her first time seeing it.

When she'd flown back for his retirement party from the force, her dad had still been looking for his first office. Taylor had gone with him to check out some possibilities, and he'd found one he liked.

When he'd brought in a partner two years ago, they'd quickly outgrown the original office space and had moved to this location.

Taylor's last trip to GraceTown was shortly before the partner and the move. The long hours demanded at the law firm in Chicago where she worked made getting away difficult.

Understanding the demands placed on a young attorney, her father traveled from Maryland to Illinois yearly to celebrate Thanksgiving and Christmas with her.

This year, she'd planned to come to GraceTown and celebrate with him. Well, it was August and she was here now, but not soon enough. The thought was a sudden knife blow to her heart. She absorbed the impact with a sharp inhale.

After taking several steadying breaths, she told herself to focus on the present.

Taylor knew the only way she could handle this difficult time was to put one foot in front of the other and do what needed to be done.

She let her gaze scan the outer office. His last office had been a hole-in-the-wall compared to this one. In addition to a partner, business had been good enough to allow him to hire a receptionist.

A desk to the right, complete with two visitor chairs, filled the small outer space.

Straight ahead were two offices: one for her dad and one for Jameson Fox. Her father's partner, a former cop, was a stranger to her. Then again, she'd also never met Glenna Kovacs, the receptionist he'd hired.

Standing there, Taylor waited for Glenna--or Jameson--to appear.

After fifteen long seconds, she called out. "Hello. Is anyone here?"

She waited another fifteen seconds before crossing to her father's office. She'd have known this was his sanctuary even without his name on the door. The clutter on top of the desk had a smile lifting her lips. She shook her head. For as long as she could remember, Bob Higgs had followed the principle that a disorganized desk was a happy desk.

No matter how cluttered his desktop looked in his home office, she'd learned that he could nip the exact paper he was looking for out of the mess at any given time.

Taylor found her gaze drawn to a pencil holder she'd made out of popsicle sticks at Brownie camp when she was eight. She'd painted each stick a different fluorescent color, then secured them around the perimeter of a soup can with Elmer's Glue. She personalized the holder by adding lots of hearts and stickers that proclaimed, "Best Dad Ever" and "I L-O-V-E my Dad."

At the time, he'd made a big deal about how much he loved the gift. Until this moment, she hadn't realized he still had it. Or the picture that sat framed on his desk. Her mother had taken it of the two of them a long-ago Halloween.

Taylor had been only five and too young to make the rounds alone. She'd dressed as Annie while her dad went as Daddy Warbucks. The dog they'd had at the time, a reddish Cockapoo named Harley, had been dubbed Sandy for the night.

Her mom—well, her mother had been designated as the one to hand out candy. She'd dressed as Miss Hannigan for the evening, wanting to feel a part of the action. They hadn't gotten a picture of the three of them together, and now she wondered why.

Taking a deep breath, Taylor picked up the pencil case. She would keep this. Looking at it would forever remind her of the wonderful father who--

"This is a private office. What do you think you're doing in here?"

Startled by the demanding deep voice, Taylor whirled. The

pencils flew right before the holder slipped from her fingers and fell to the floor, several sticks coming loose from the can.

Taylor let out a little cry at the sight of the popsicle sticks scattered at her feet. Telling herself she had more important things to worry about right now, she lifted her gaze to see two strangers in the doorway.

"Who are you?" This question, containing more puzzlement than anger, came from the mid-fifties woman beside the man.

The woman's oversized glasses gave her face an owl-like appearance. Her curly brown hair sprang out from her head as if she'd just stuck her finger in a light socket.

The man beside her, who she pegged as close to her own age, was tall and broad-shouldered with dark hair cut stylishly short. Right now, he gazed at her with suspicious dark eyes. "What are you doing in Bob's office?"

Taylor kept her eyes on both as she bent over and scooped up the popsicle sticks, placing them in the can. "I could ask you the same."

"We work here." The man spoke cooly. "Your turn."

"You're Jameson Fox."

Why had she thought he'd be older?

"You know my name." His eyes never left her face. His voice, while calm and polite, held an undercurrent of steel. "Now tell me yours."

The tone demanded rather than asked for a response.

"Taylor Higgs." Realizing she was making a mess of this first encounter, she smiled and struck out her hand. "Sorry for the misunderstanding. I'm Bob's daughter. It's good to meet you finally."

"Taylor. Oh my goodness." Rushing forward, the woman quickly closed the distance to Taylor before catching her in a tight embrace. "I'm so happy to meet you. We loved your dad so much."

If he was Jameson, this was likely Glenna Kovacs, the receptionist. Her father had teasingly referred to Glenna as his work wife since she handled so much around the office.

Since he'd often mentioned Glenna in his texts and Facetime chats, Taylor wondered if something more personal was happening between her dad and the woman.

He hadn't said, and she hadn't asked. Taylor figured those were the kinds of questions best asked in person.

As Glenna squeezed tight and the scent of Gardenia wrapped around Taylor, for an instant, she let herself lean.

Then Taylor stepped back and gave Glenna a watery smile. "I can't believe he's gone."

Jameson, who'd bent over to scoop up the pencils, straightened and set them on the corner of her father's desk. "It was a shock to everyone."

"I didn't get many details." Taylor shifted her gaze from Jameson to Glenna.

"Bob had been complaining of a headache for about a week." Jameson's lips tightened momentarily before he continued. "We urged him to see a doctor. He said he would when he had time."

"He was fine that morning when he left on surveillance. No complaints about the headache, remember?" Glenna shot a glance at Jameson before returning her attention to Taylor. "Your dad said he'd be back by noon. The three of us ate lunch together on Monday."

"Over lunch, we'd have our staff meeting," Jameson added.

He'd shoved his hands into his pockets and rocked back on his heels.

"It was nearly twelve when I noticed him sitting in his car out front. The sun was bright, and I couldn't see him very well. I assumed he was finishing up a call." Glenna blinked rapidly. "Finally, at about twelve-fifteen, I went out to see what was taking him so long. Th-that's when I-I found him."

Glenna turned to Jameson, her face awash with misery. "I still keep thinking if I'd gone out sooner, maybe--"

"He was already gone." Jameson's arm stole around her shoulder.

"But if—" Glenna began again.

"We've talked about this before," Jameson reminded her. "The doctor said he didn't have a chance, no matter when he was found."

"That's what I was told." Taylor heard herself say. She'd initially ignored the call from an unfamiliar number when it had come through. But, after listening to the message left, she'd called back. That's when she received the devastating news.

Her father, an active and fit fifty-eight-year-old with his whole life ahead of him, had passed away from a ruptured brain aneurysm.

If bad things did come in threes, she'd had her quota.

Only a few days before she'd gotten the call about her dad, she'd been given her walking papers from the firm she'd worked for since graduating from law school. The firm was acquired by another, and she was deemed a redundant employee. The fact that she wasn't the only one let go didn't provide much comfort.

Especially when her boyfriend, who had been kept on, broke up with her, citing it wouldn't look good for him to be dating someone who'd been terminated.

Both of those events, though, paled in comparison to losing her father. Bob Higgs was her daddy, her rock, the one person that she trusted to always be there for her.

From the time Taylor had been small, her dad had told her she could count on him always being in her back pocket, close by whenever she needed him.

Now, he was gone.

"Taylor."

The sound of her name pulled her from her reverie. Two sets of eyes were staring at her.

"I'm sorry." Taylor rubbed her hand across her face. "This past week has been incredibly difficult."

Because there would be no job to return to, instead of immediately flying to GraceTown, Taylor had taken a week to settle things in Chicago.

Her roommate Angi had been happy that Taylor could move out and thrilled when she said she'd be leaving her furniture behind. Angi's boyfriend had already begun moving in before Taylor had finished packing.

"I assume you're here to plan the funeral." Glenna offered Taylor a supportive smile. "I've been making a list of possible music and service details, things I thought Bob would like and—"

"Thank you for that, but I'm going to put that off for now."

Glenna took a step back, unable to hide her surprise. "Pardon me?"

"Dad wasn't a big fan of traditional funerals." Taylor ran a tongue across her suddenly dry lips. "I believe he'd prefer a memorial service over a funeral. Actually, I don't think he'd want anything."

"What?" Glenna's voice rose, then broke. "Are you saying... that doesn't seem—"

Jameson's hand on Glenna's arm had her stopping mid-sentence. "Taylor is Bob's next of kin. It's her decision, not ours."

"I plan to schedule a memorial service," Taylor hastened to reassure them. "I just need time."

"Of course." Jameson offered her a reassuring smile. "Whatever you need, we're here to help. Aren't we, Glenna?"

"Yes, absolutely." Glenna took a deep breath and appeared to steady. "When do you need to be back in Chicago?"

"I'm staying in GraceTown for now. I have an appointment with my dad's attorney. Once I speak with him, that will give me a better idea of where I am going forward."

"Take all the time you need." A look of sympathy filled Glenna's eyes. "I'm sure you know this, but I'll say it anyway: your dad was incredibly proud of you. He loved you very much."

"Bob was a good man," Jameson added. "The best."

Truer words, Taylor thought.

As grief once again rolled over her in a black wave, the best she could muster was a jerky nod.

+

Jameson watched Taylor step out into the bright summer sun. She was far prettier than the woman he had visualized when Bob spoke of her, which was often.

He wasn't sure why, but he'd assumed she looked like her dad —a short, stocky man with wiry black hair and a sharp jawline.

The only thing Jameson could figure, now that he'd seen the tall, willowy blonde with the big brown eyes, was that she must take after her mother, a woman he'd never met.

According to what little Bob had said, he and his ex-wife had split when Taylor was in high school. When the ex moved to California after the divorce, Taylor stayed in GraceTown.

Bob, the kindest man Jameson had ever met, was also an excellent judge of character. Despite Taylor not having been back to see her dad, at least not since Jameson had become Bob's partner, Bob had loved his daughter deeply, which meant she was a good person.

Because family or not, Bob was nobody's fool.

"I didn't recognize her," Glenna spoke matter-of-factly, even as her eyes lingered on the empty chair behind Bob's desk.

Jameson lifted his hands and spread his fingers. "Not surprising. She was just a kid in the photo on Bob's desk."

In the photo, she's dressed in an Orphan Annie Halloween costume, complete with a red yarn wig and face paint. Bob has made an interesting-looking Daddy Warbucks.

"I know she wants to do what's right for her father, but we should be planning his service," Glenna continued. "We're the ones who've been here for him, not her."

Jameson shook his head. While he understood Glenna's perspective—she'd always been fiercely protective of Bob—in this situation, friends weren't the same as family. "Bob would want her to handle this."

Glenna's brows drew together. "You think?"

"I know." The only thing that surprised him was that Glenna didn't.

"What about the business?"

Jameson stilled. "What about it?"

"You and Bob were partners." Returning to the chair behind her desk, Glenna dropped down and swiveled the chair back and forth, her eyes never leaving his face. "What do you want to bet that Bob left her his share?"

"Maybe." It would have been unexpected if Bob had left him the business, but occasionally, long shots did come in. He shrugged. "If he did, I'm sure she'll sell it to me. What good is it to her?"

"You're probably right." Glenna's voice softened. "Do you have the money to buy her out? If not, I have some savings. I'd be happy to lend you some."

"That's a generous offer, and I appreciate it." This conversation ventured as close to personal as Glenna had gotten with him. Though she was constantly butting into Bob's business, a fact Bob appeared to enjoy, she'd stayed out of his.

Jameson hoped that wouldn't change now that Bob was gone. Still, he wouldn't take Glenna's money. She'd worked hard for whatever savings she'd accumulated, which made her offer that much sweeter.

"As long as she doesn't think Bob's share is worth a fortune, I should have enough."

"Okay, then." Glenna picked up the brown bag she'd dropped on Bob's desk when they entered the office and saw a strange woman beside it.

"Back to business." Glenna gestured to her clean and tidy desktop. "Do you want to eat out here?"

"What say we skip the meeting this week? We could maybe do it once we organize a few things and know better where we're at."

"Works for me."

"Good. I have some calls to make. I'll take my food and eat at my desk."

"I'll do the same." Glenna expelled a shaky breath. "No surprise. I haven't got much work done this past week."

Jameson understood. Both he and Glenna had been floundering since that horrible day.

Glenna took out the sandwiches, chips, and brownie squares they'd purchased from a food truck parked down the block.

"I was thinking that the next time we decide to leave the office at the same time, we need to lock up." The thought of locking up hadn't crossed his mind since they'd been just down the street and only gone for ten minutes max. "I don't know about you, but it was a shock to see someone in here. Especially in Bob's office."

Glenna shook her head. "I wasn't sure what to think, but I'm on board. The front door really does need to be locked unless one of us is here."

Leaning over, Jameson scooped up his share of the food truck lunch. When he straightened, he found Glenna staring, a speculative gleam in her eyes. "She's a pretty one, isn't she?"

"She's lovely." He smiled, recalling how her long, honey-blonde hair had been tousled around her shoulders as if she'd hopped out of bed with no time to brush it. Her large dark brown eyes had been an enchanting contrast to the lightness of her hair.

"I wonder if she's dating anyone." Glenna brought two fingers to her lips and tapped them against her mouth. "I would think if she was and it was serious, he'd have come with her."

"It doesn't matter." Jameson kept his tone easy, knowing that

Glenna's predilection for matchmaking wouldn't have a chance to get started this time. "Once things get settled here, I bet neither of us will ever see her again."

This absolutely gripping story will keep you turning the page way too late at night. Grab your copy now!

ALSO BY CINDY KIRK

Good Hope Series

The Good Hope series is a must-read for those who love stories that
uplift and bring a smile to your face.

GraceTown Series

Enchanting stories that are a perfect mixture of romance, friendship, and
magical moments set in a community known for unexplainable
happenings.

Hazel Green Series

These heartwarming stories, set in the tight-knit community of Hazel
Green, are sure to move you, uplift you, inspire and delight you. Enjoy
uplifting romances that will keep you turning the page!

Holly Pointe Series

Readers say "If you are looking for a festive, romantic read this
Christmas, these are the books for you."

Jackson Hole Series

Heartwarming and uplifting stories set in beautiful Jackson Hole,
Wyoming.

Silver Creek Series

Engaging and heartfelt romances centered around two powerful families
whose fortunes were forged in the Colorado silver mines.

Sweet River Montana Series

A community serving up a slice of small-town Montana life, where helping hands abound and people fall in love in the context of home and family.

Made in the USA
Columbia, SC
24 May 2025